"I want to apologize for everything in the past. How I behaved."

He cringed thinking of the last time he'd seen that pretty face of hers; she'd been crying. The last thing he'd heard her say in that husky voice of hers was "You're leaving because I thought I was pregnant, aren't you?"

"I'm sorry Maddie," he repeated.

"Apology accepted. In return, I'd like your promise you won't bring up our past again. We need to concentrate on helping people here. Are you capable of that? Because if you're not, this will never work."

"I'm capable of that," he returned, offended. "Obviously we've both gotten on with our lives."

"Yes, we have. Best you remember that, Nick."

"I will, Dr. Walsh."

Although he wasn't sure he could…because it was a lie.

Dear Reader,

Welcome to one of my favorite Harlequin Superromance novels. The idea for this story came to me in two parts. Every summer I work at a camp for kids with cancer. Our group meets to wait for the bus at the Crime Victims Resource Center in my hometown. The place is in a beautiful old brick building in the heart of the city, and houses organizations that help the victims of crimes. I thought, "What a great place this is. And there would be so many story lines for a novel." I couldn't get the idea out of my mind all year.

So when I finished *Tell Me No Lies,* which had Nick Logan, the hero's brother, as a teen counselor, I promptly moved him to Rockford, New York, where his brother relocates, and gave Nick his own story. (No need to read his brother's book first, though, as this one stands alone.)

The Rockford Crime Victims' Center, is self-contained, not just a resource center, based on similar national operations. The people at these centers do wonderful work, helping those victimized by crime with the emotional, legal and practical ramifications. Because of my background as a teacher, and my love for helping kids, I made Nick the counselor for teenagers. Their situations are heartbreaking, but very real. And, of course, Nick is able to make great strides with them.

Nick also ends up working with Madelyn, a woman he broke up with three years before. And she's now his boss. They hate working together, opening old wounds and resurrecting old feelings, but they'll do anything for kids, which makes them immensely admirable to me. And yes, in the course of helping two troubled teens, Nick and Maddie find a way to overcome their differences and past hurts.

I love to hear from readers. E-mail me at kshay@rochester.rr.com or write to me at P.O. Box 24288, Rochester, NY 14624. And please visit my Web site and blog at www.kathrynshay.com, and the Superromance site at www.superauthors.com.

Kathryn Shay

THE WRONG MAN
FOR HER
Kathryn Shay

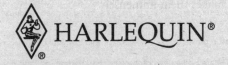

HARLEQUIN®

TORONTO • NEW YORK • LONDON
AMSTERDAM • PARIS • SYDNEY • HAMBURG
STOCKHOLM • ATHENS • TOKYO • MILAN • MADRID
PRAGUE • WARSAW • BUDAPEST • AUCKLAND

ISBN-13: 978-0-373-71418-6
ISBN-10: 0-373-71418-1

THE WRONG MAN FOR HER

www.eHarlequin.com

Printed in U.S.A.

ABOUT THE AUTHOR

Kathryn Shay is the author of twenty-one Harlequin Superromance books and seven novels and two novellas from the Berkley Publishing Group. She has won several awards. Among them are five *Romantic Times BOOKreviews* awards, three Holt Medallions, three Desert Quill awards and the Booksellers' Best Award. A former high school teacher, she lives in upstate New York, where she sets many of her stories.

Books by Kathryn Shay

HARLEQUIN SUPERROMANCE

This book is for people all over the world who dedicate their lives to helping others.

CHAPTER ONE

NICK LOGAN SLAMMED on the brakes of his little red Mitsubishi Eclipse. Too late. The front end rammed into the back of the van ahead of him. *Damn it!* Though he'd only glanced away from the snarl of traffic to check the clock, it had been enough time for the long line of vehicles snaking down Route 390 to come to an abrupt halt.

"Great," he said, unbuckling the seat belt. "Just great." He vaulted out of the car and hurried to the driver's side of the van.

Behind the wheel, a man in a business suit had a cell phone to his ear. The guy said something into the mouthpiece, closed the instrument and stuffed it into his pocket. He finally opened the door and got out. "What the hell did you do?"

Nick refrained from reminding him that using a cell phone while driving in New York State was illegal. "You stopped fast. I hit you. Are you all right?"

"No, I'm not all right." The man's face flushed. "I have an important meeting in thirty minutes, and I don't have time for this." He pointed to his van. "Or this." He gestured toward the traffic around them.

"Me, either." The last thing Nick needed was to be late for his first day on the job. Well, his first day *back* on the job. He glanced at the two bumpers. "I think I took the brunt of it."

The man strode to the rear of the van and whistled. "That's what you get for going foreign. And buying a sports car."

"Whatever." Nick hated lectures. "How do you want to handle this?"

"You'll pay, of course."

"I mean, do you want to call the police or take care of this privately?"

The driver raised his brows. "Can you afford the cash outlay? The cost of your repair is going to be steep, even if it's just a crumpled bumper."

"Probably not." Nick wasn't thinking clearly. He'd been up pacing the floor most of the night, worried about returning to his old job after a three-year absence. He whipped out his cell. "I'll call."

The guy surveyed the traffic. "They won't be able to get through."

"The cops'll find us." They always did. Nick knew that from personal experience.

"I..."

The wind picked up around them, along with a fine March drizzle. Oh, man, this just kept getting worse. As he punched in 9-1-1, Nick hoped like hell his lousy morning didn't foreshadow the rest of the day. At least he'd given himself an hour-and-a-half leeway before his meeting with John. And his good friend would be an understanding boss. Or he used to be, anyway.

It took close to sixty minutes for the police to arrive, deal with the reports and for Nick to exchange information with the other driver. It took another twenty to get out of the heavy traffic, which had worsened because of the accident.

He pulled into the Rockford Crime Victims Center parking lot at nine. His need for haste kept him from succumbing to the memories that swamped him as he took in the old, brick building on Plymouth Avenue. He shoved aside any feelings of nostalgia at being back at the Center, where he'd spent several years doing a job that helped other people and made him feel worthwhile.

It was also the place where he'd fallen in love. Though at the time, he wouldn't admit it to himself. Or to Maddie. At least she wasn't working here anymore. He didn't know where she was now, or even if she was still in Rockford. He'd made sure, whenever he'd seen John over the past three years, or exchanged e-mails with Bethany, the Center's part-time minister, that they didn't discuss Maddie. All he'd learned was that she'd left the RCVC shortly after he had and had gone on to graduate school. Today, there would only be painful reminders of her within those walls.

The entrance door was unlocked and the reception

area was empty. Nick knew Francy Baker, the Center's secretary, still worked here so perhaps the staff meeting had started. He headed to John's office on the first floor to check where he was supposed to be.

The door was ajar.

Nick stopped short when he heard the voice that had haunted so many of his midnights say, "It's past nine. Do you think he's coming?"

Maddie. His Maddie? *What the hell?*

"Yes, of course." John sounded weary. "Today's his first day as the teen counselor. I'm surprised he's late."

Nick stepped into the entrance. "I'm here."

When Maddie faced him, his pulse sped up. This was his first sight of her since that cold November night three years, four months and two weeks ago when he'd broken off their relationship. She'd changed. Her dark blond hair was shorter now, falling over her eyes in cute bangs. And she wasn't smiling at him.

He tried to calm his thumping heart. "Hi, Madelyn. John. Sorry I'm late." He shrugged one shoulder. "Car accident."

"Hey, buddy." Rising from a chair, John Kramer, the founder and head of the RCVC, circled around the desk. Without hesitation, he gave Nick a bear hug. When he drew back, he held Nick by the arms. John's hair was grayer than the last time Nick had seen him, and he looked exhausted. "You okay? Anybody hurt?"

"Only the front of my car. At least it's still drivable." He glanced at Maddie, then dropped into a chair when she did the same. John went back to his desk. "What's going on?" Nick asked. "Why are you here, Maddie? I was under the impression you left the Center a few years ago."

John sat forward. "Nick, some things have happened you need to know about. Things that have brought Maddie back to the RCVC."

"What?"

"Lucy had a heart attack six weeks ago."

Nick recoiled. "Oh, no. H-how is she?"

"Recovered, miraculously. I took the month off to be with her."

"I see." Relief came quickly and, on the heels of it, a glimmer of understanding. "So Maddie filled in for you?"

"In a sense." He cleared his throat. "My wife's illness shocked me into admitting some things. Ever since my daughter died, I've devoted my entire life to this place and neglected other important aspects. It's time to focus on them now."

"Well, that's good. I told you before you needed to slow down."

Something wasn't right here, though. He and John had kept in touch since he'd left the Center and it was unusual for them to go six weeks without talking. Of course, Nick had spent the past few months rearranging his life to move back up to Rockford. Still, given how close he was to the Kramers, he was surprised John hadn't told him about something this serious. "Why didn't you call me about Lucy? I could have come up early to help at the Center. Or to support you two, at least."

John glanced at Maddie. "I was afraid if you knew my circumstances you wouldn't accept the job."

"Why? Because you won't be running the place?"

"Yes, though I'll be here part-time. And will still do your evaluations. But I'm no longer in charge."

"I don't understand. Won't the new administrator…" His words trailed off as awareness dawned. He looked to Maddie, whose stricken face confirmed his suspicions. "You're the new administrator of the Center."

"Yes, I am. I took over for John a month ago and I'm staying on to run it."

"Permanently?"

"Yes."

Nick gripped the chair. It took him several seconds to rein in his resentment at being duped—by both of them. He struggled to control his anger only because John didn't need a tirade now. Choosing his words carefully, he addressed his friend and mentor. "I'd like to speak to Madelyn alone, if you don't mind."

"This isn't her fault, Nick. I made the decision to keep you in the dark. As I said, I was afraid you wouldn't come back if you knew Maddie was in charge."

"It's okay, John." Maddie's voice was calm. Of course, she'd had time to adjust to this very bad idea. "I'd like to talk to Nick, too. Alone."

Sighing, John stood. "All right. But if anyone's to blame, it's me. Meanwhile I'll go to the staff meeting and tell everybody you'll be along shortly."

When John circled around the desk, Nick rose, too, and grasped his arm. Ignoring the hurt caused by the fact that the Kramers had shut him out, he said, "Don't worry about this, John. Just take care of Lucy."

After John left, Nick turned and anchored his hands on the back of the chair. "Surely you must know this can never work."

Her amber eyes flared, making them look like hot brandy. "No, I don't know that. I wouldn't have taken the job if I didn't think we could do this."

"Why the hell *did* you take it?"

"For the same reason you just assured John everything would work out. He's lost too much in his life and now he has a personal crisis. We have to help out."

"Madelyn, you can't want to work with me."

"Of course I don't!" She slapped her pad down on the desk. "We might as well get everything out in the open. I never would have hired you back if I'd been in charge when John offered you the job. But that would have been a real loss to the Center, since you work magic with kids. It's right for you to be here, so we'll have to make the best of the fact that we have an unpleasant past together."

His grip tightened on the chair. Her compliment didn't ease his anger. "It is *not* acceptable that I wasn't told about Lucy's attack or that *you'd* be running the Center!"

She just stared at him. He could see the strain around her mouth and the tension in her jaw, but she held her ground.

"Damn it," he said, "what am I supposed to do now?"

"Stay. For the Center's sake and John's."

"And if I do?" He practically spat the words out. "What about *us?*"

"There is no *us,* any longer. Right now, we have to think about the victims we can help and what we can do for the Kramers. They were like parents to both of us. We owe them a lot."

The mention of the role the Kramers had played in Nick's life diluted some of his rage. Okay, so he should stay at the Center. Hell, he wanted to. But, man, he hadn't signed on for *this.* He wasn't sure he could do it. Yet, did he really have a choice? "I guess I can give it a shot."

"Fine." She glanced at her watch and stood. "The staff is probably finished with doughnuts and coffee. We should get down there."

"Wait a second, Maddie."

She straightened her shoulders. "Please, don't call me that."

"What?"

"Maddie."

"Why?"

She raised an eyebrow, and he remembered that only he, Beth and John had ever used the nickname. For some reason, her admonition ticked him off.

He folded his arms over his chest. "Would you prefer Dr. Walsh?"

"*Madelyn* is fine." Without saying more, she turned and headed out the door.

Rattled by the events of the morning, he followed her. Holy hell, could things get any worse?

UNDER THE conference room table, Madelyn gripped her pen and tried to take surreptitious deep breaths. Her voice was even when she said, "Hi, everyone. Sorry we're late."

She nodded to Nick, who'd casually sat down in an unoccupied seat at the other end of table, as if he was merely some new employee. Her pounding heart told her differently. It didn't help that he looked better than ever in his navy sports coat, silk T-shirt and khaki pants; his dark hair fell boyishly over his navy blue eyes. But she'd be damned if she'd reveal her personal reaction to him.

"Some of you, of course, will remember Nick. Those of you who don't, this is Nick Logan. He's a psychotherapist, with an undergrad degree in social work and a masters in psychology, specializing in teenagers. He worked at the RCVC for six years then left for a while. He's back now and is heading up our new teen division. Hiring him was John's last formal act as director." She gave everyone a forced smile. "Let's start today by introducing ourselves. Those of you who don't know Nick can fill him in on what you do here."

At her left, John waved. "Hey, there. Glad you're back, Nick. It means a lot to me."

"It's good to be here." Nobody else would know from his tone of voice, but a little muscle leaped in his jaw telling Madelyn he was anything but happy.

"I'm in-and-out, periodically, and I'm still writing the grants," John continued. "I guess I couldn't quit altogether."

"You have a lot invested." Madelyn smiled affectionately at John. "I'm thankful for whatever time you can give us."

She nodded to the next person. Francy greeted Nick and welcomed him back, as did Abe Carpenter and Deanna Gomez, the counselors for adults. Madelyn knew that both Abe and Deanna liked and respected Nick.

"Hi, Nick. I'm Reid Taylor. I came a few months after you left. I'm a social worker and in charge of the new hotline. I also head the education division. I'm sure we'll be working together on school programs."

On Reid's left, Connor Worthington absently straightened his tie. Classically handsome with dark blond hair and somewhat cold gray eyes, he introduced himself as the lawyer on board.

Nick studied the other man. "We have full-time legal help now?"

Connor said no more, just nodded, so Madelyn explained. "The New York State Bar Association voted to give specially selected organizations like ours a grant for legal aid. Connor's been with us for six months. We also have a lawyer who helps us out pro bono, but since she's a volunteer she doesn't make many staff meetings."

Madelyn nodded to Emma Jones to continue the introductions. "Hello, Nick. I don't know if you remember me. I started volunteering a few weeks before you left and am now coordinating all the Center's volunteers. Welcome back." She gave him a brief rundown on the people at the RCVC who donated their time to do everything from office work, to court accompaniment, to child care when victims went to their myriad appointments.

"Our police rep isn't able to be here today." Madelyn finished up with, "And neither is Bethany Hunter. Her son is ill. You remember her, of course."

Their part-time minister who oversaw all faith-based initiatives was also Madelyn's best friend, even though Beth had maintained contact with Nick after he left town. The fact that her calming presence wouldn't be around today had worried Madelyn till dawn, when she'd finally given up on sleep and come here.

Madelyn gestured to Joe, a paramedic who worked at the Center two days a week. "Logan," Joe said curtly. "Never expected to see you back here."

There was a brief, uncomfortable moment of silence. Joe's tone of voice could not be misinterpreted. Only Madelyn, John and Nick knew the reason for his hostility.

Nick's gaze zeroed in on Joe, and a bit of the old

street kid Nick used to be surfaced from beneath the sophisticated exterior. "I bet you didn't. But the chance to head a newly funded teen division was an offer I couldn't refuse." He stared hard at Joe. "Still advising on insurance forms and medical issues?"

"Yep. I also teach self-defense classes a couple times a week."

Madelyn jumped in. "I guess that's it for introductions. Nick, you can meet the people who aren't here and catch up on what they do later. You and I will have more time to talk after the meeting." She glanced at her agenda, though she knew it by heart. "I've tried to keep this short." She held up a blue paper. "Schedules are due today by three. Leave them with Francy. If you have any questions, see me. I'll be in my office until five forty-five, except for a meeting with the mayor at eleven."

Nick frowned down at the paper, then up at her. "What schedules?"

"Since our hours vary according to need, counseling sessions, court visits, et cetera, on Monday I get a schedule of what everyone will be doing that week."

He tossed the paper aside. "I won't be able to fill this out."

"Why?"

"I don't meet with the kids until Wednesday. I won't know their requirements until then, which will determine what I do. And I'll be off-site a lot when I go to their schools."

"You'll have to run all that by me."

"Why?"

"Because it's protocol." She winced at the edge in her voice and the vagueness of the comment. "Look, I have to know where everyone is so I can find people if they're needed by clients. And when emergencies arise."

Irritation flared in his face. "I see. Anything else new?"

A few of the staff snickered.

"What?"

Francy shook her head. "The reactions are in reference to the luncheon support group we have every Friday."

"For the clients?"

"No, for the staff."

"You're kidding, right?"

"No," John said, "she isn't. It's something I wholly endorse. The National Crime Prevention Bureau recommends personal reflection and support groups for all employees who work at centers like this."

Nick ran a hand though his dark hair, disheveling it. "Is participation optional?"

"No."

"Any other policies I should know about?"

Maddie raised her chin. "Some. But we don't need to review them as a group, since you're the only newbie. As I said, I'll fill you in at the end of the meeting. Today's agenda includes updates on the grant for a part-time counselor for the teen support group, some new reporting forms from the state and the week-long training at the New York State Victims Academy in Buffalo this summer. We also need to talk about the plans for National Crime Victims' Rights Week coming up in April." During which John will be honored in Washington, D.C., with the Award for Professional Innovation in Victim Services. "Want to start with that, Francy, since this year's so special for us?"

Nick held up his hand. "Wait a second. A part-time counselor for my kids?"

"Yes. We don't run any groups of six or more with one counselor anymore."

"I work alone."

"Not in the group sessions. Of course you'll meet individually with each kid by yourself, but policy dictates you'll have someone else in the group with you." Madelyn could tell he wasn't happy, so she tried to be professional. "Nick, think about it. With someone else assisting you, you'll have more face time with the kids and more help with the paperwork. And everyone knows the smaller the ratio of kids to adults, the better the sessions go."

He stared at her, his jaw clenched. When he didn't say anything more, she told Francy to begin. As the secretary handed out a memo on the National Crime Victims' Rights Week, Madelyn glanced at the clock. She kept these meetings to an hour, if possible. Only forty-five minutes to go, then she'd have to deal with Nick's objections to her policies, to her style of management. To her.

So be it. She'd faced worse. Like climbing out of the morass of poverty all by herself. Like recovering from her own victimization. Like getting over Nick Logan when he dumped her three years ago. She'd handle his return to the Center with equal efficiency and success.

Even if it killed her.

"WOULD YOU LIKE a break before we meet?" Maddie's tone was clipped, giving Nick an indication of how their private meeting was going to unfold. They were the only ones left in the conference room.

"No, thanks. I have a lot to do before my first session with the kids."

Folding her arms over her chest, she faced him squarely. "Which you *will* run by me."

Okay, so he'd make the first move. He stood, walked down to her end and took an adjacent chair. "Maddie…Madelyn, what's going on? It sounds like I have to tell you everything I plan to do."

"You have a problem with running things by me?"

"The problem is, I was hired to *head* the teen division."

"I'm your boss, Nick."

"Technically. But we both know I was brought here unaware of that fact." She opened her mouth to speak, but he held up his hand. "No, let me finish. You're right, I owe it to John to stay. I *want* to help him out. And truthfully, this is an ideal job for me. But John assured me I'd be given carte blanche here."

"John assured *me* you weren't going to fly solo on this."

"Are you assigning another counselor to my group because you don't trust me? Because our counseling styles are different?"

"No, I meant it when I said I think it's better for the kids. The other counselors agree." She studied him. "You have a tough group there, Nick. I've already met with each of them. You'll need all the help you can get."

"I've read their files." He planned to have them memorized by the time he met with the kids.

"Then you know what's ahead of you."

"Who's the other counselor?"

"I'm not sure. I have three people interested, but I have to get the funding before I can hire someone. I'm expecting confirmation today."

"Maybe it won't come through," he said almost to himself.

"I hope it does. Don't forget, you'll be doing more than counseling. You've got to oversee the kids' legal situations, restitution and a whole slew of other details."

"There are people working here who take care of those areas."

"But you have to determine what those people need to do and make sure that everything is being done. Your job involves a lot of juggling."

He shook his head.

She stared at him. "You're going to have to learn

to play nice with others, Nick. No matter how much you need to keep that personal shield around you."

He hadn't expected a dig so soon, especially after she'd asked him to stay. "Is that what this is all about, our former relationship?"

"No." Her face reddened. "And don't ever accuse me of that again."

He drummed his fingers on the table. "Look, I don't want to argue with you."

"We aren't arguing. You'll have another counselor in the group with you, period. And I'm entitled to know your plans for the kids, what you're doing, how it's going."

"You want to know, or approve my plans?"

She sighed heavily. "I'm sure there won't be much disagreement between us about those things. We do have different styles, as you say, but I never opposed yours when we worked together before. I don't know why you think I would now."

Leaning back in the chair, he tried to appear relaxed and confident. "All right. I'll agree to that. But I'm not coming to the staff support group." Surely she'd let him off this one. She knew how hard it was for him to open up, damn it. He'd only recently been able to talk about his feelings with his brother Dan and sister-in-law, Tessa. His close relationship with them was one of the reasons he'd come to Rockford when they'd decided to relocate here.

"You have no choice in that, either."

"It's not my thing, Maddie."

"If you've read the psychology journals lately you know that having a staff support group prevents burnout and alleviates stress. I'm not flying by the seat of my pants on this, Nick. And for the record, I'm well aware of your personality. This, however, is nonnegotiable." She drew in a breath and seemed to collect herself. "You can pass on the personal stuff if you have to."

"Personal stuff?"

"Each week we share a professional success and challenge and a personal success and challenge."

"Oh, great."

"It *is* great. After the first few meetings, the staff voted unanimously to keep the sessions going."

He stared at her.

"And I provide lunch. Sometimes I even cook."

"That's a switch. When we were together, you could barely boil water. I cooked for you all the time."

"I take cooking classes. And please don't refer to our personal relationship."

"Why? Your subtext is referring to it all the time." When she didn't respond, he watched her. "How are you, really?"

Her intense gaze never wavered from his. "I'm good, Nick, really good." She stood. "I'll show you your office." She gestured around the room. "This is where you'll hold your support groups."

Nick studied the formal space with its dark cherry paneling and furniture. "Unacceptable."

She sighed, exasperated. "Why?"

"I can't hold a support group here for kids. It has no teen atmosphere."

Her eyes sparked with interest this time.

"We need a place to call ours. Teen-friendly furniture, posters on the wall, books and materials spread around. I'll also need a fridge for snacks, personal journals for each kid, arts and crafts materials."

"Sounds like you have things all planned out."

"As you said, I know what I'm doing."

"Yes, of course you do."

"Is my office big enough to turn into a group room?"

She thought for a minute. "We can do better than that. Come on, I'll show you a storage area that you can use. It'll need some work, though it does have big windows."

"Thanks. For giving in on this."

"I'm not giving in. I never had any intention of blocking good ideas. I will not, however, let you steamroll me."

"Of course you won't."

She started to gather her papers.

"I'd like to say one more thing."

"What?"

"I, um, want to apologize for everything that happened in the past. How I behaved." He cringed, thinking of the last time he'd seen that pretty face of hers; it had been awash with tears. The last thing he'd heard that husky voice say was, *You're leaving because I thought I was pregnant, aren't you?* "I'm sorry, Maddie."

"Apology accepted. In return, I'd like your promise not to bring up our past again. We need to concentrate on helping people here. Are you capable of doing that? Because if you're not, this will never work."

For some reason, he felt offended. "I'm capable of doing that. Obviously, we've both gone on with our lives."

"Yes, we have. Best you remember that, Nick."

"I will, Dr. Walsh."

CHAPTER TWO

"WATCH OUT THERE, beautiful, you're up damn high."

Tessa smiled down at Nick from the ladder, which allowed her to reach the twelve-foot ceiling of his newly designated group session room.

"Because you're afraid of heights, doesn't mean everyone is." Tessa giggled at his phobia. It was good to see his sister-in-law happy after the trouble she and his brother had last summer. A man from her past had stalked her and ended up dead. The scandal almost destroyed their marriage. "Anyway, it makes you human."

"Oh, I'm all too human." He tapped the side of the paint can. "You sure about this color?"

"The kids will like it. Blue is soothing, makes people more relaxed. Its deep shade won't be too prissy for teenagers." She scanned the area she'd already done. "The four windows are great and there's enough room for the kids to sprawl out. But maybe we could have waited for them to pick out the color."

"No, I'll let them choose what stuff to put up on the walls. I want them to feel welcome here at the first session. Lucky me that you had today off and could help paint." He glanced at his watch. "I'm expecting the furniture tonight, so we'd better get going."

Roller in hand, he began to slather paint on the parts of the wall he could reach, while Tessa cut in from the top. They made small talk as they worked. "Everything going well at the Villa?" he asked.

Tessa had taken a job as a librarian at a local teen detention center. Much like him, she worked well with troubled kids because she'd been one herself.

"Couldn't be better. I got a grant from the New York State Arts Foundation for more books and am itching to spend it."

"I'd be interested in what you're ordering. I was hoping to have some teen lit in here."

"I could do some research into adolescent literature about victimization." She cocked her head. "One author I know of is David Pelzer."

"Yeah, his books are gruesome enough to snag the kids' attention." Pelzer had been abused by his mother for years and vividly recounted his experiences in his writing.

"He's coming to town for Crime Victims' Rights Week."

"Really?" Nick said. "Nobody told me about it. Then again, nobody told me about a lot of things."

"The Villa clients are going. Your kids probably can, too."

From the corner, soft rock drifted out from the CD player as they continued their task.

"What did you mean, nobody told you about a lot of things?" Tessa asked.

He hesitated. "Madelyn's back at the Center."

Tessa stopped painting and looked down at him. *"What?"*

When she and Dan had put pressure on him to move to Rockford, Nick had confessed to them what had happened between him and Maddie. God, he hated to talk about his failures, even with people who loved him.

He also explained about John and Lucy.

"I'm so sorry. I know how close you are to them. Is Lucy all right?"

"Yes, but John's easing off on his work here because of her."

"That must have been a hard decision for him to make."

Tessa was right about that. John's daughter, Zoe, had been beaten and raped, then shot to death twenty years ago. The Kramer family had practically fallen apart and there'd been no organizations to help them out. After they'd begun to heal, John had vowed to do something in Zoe's memory for other crime victims' families, as well as for the victims themselves.

Nick smiled, proud of the fact that, two decades later, the Kramer Group, which eventually became the Rockford Crime Victims Center, was one of the most renowned victim assistance organizations in the state.

"It gets worse, Tessa."

"How?"

"Madelyn's my boss."

This time, she climbed down from the ladder. "Oh, Nick. How on earth is that going to work?"

"It has to. John needs us both and you know how I feel about abandoning people."

"I guess." Her expression was trouble. "How is Madelyn?"

"Distant." He rolled harder, faster. "In *charge!*"

"Damn. We wanted you to come to Rockford with us, but working with her won't be easy."

"I can't believe it." He set the roller down and whipped off his overshirt, revealing a ragged University of Rockford T-shirt. "She wants to check everything I do."

"Well, you can't blame her, if she runs the place now." Tessa picked up her bottle of water and sipped from it. She looked about twenty in her jeans, T-shirt and curly hair, though she was thirty-eight, his age.

"Tell me about it. Her new policy also dictates I work with another counselor in the support group. I'm trying to block that."

Tessa's gaze focused on him.

"What?"

"Do you think that's best for the kids?"

He crossed to the fridge Maddie had gotten for him yesterday afternoon and retrieved a bottle of soda. "You think I'm being unreasonable?"

Tessa dropped to the floor and patted the space beside her. "Sit." When he joined her, she said,

"Two people to help eight clients? You can play off each other's observations. Talk things over. Seems ideal to me."

"That's what Maddie said." He peeled back the label on the bottle with his thumbnail. "I hope my judgment hasn't clouded by my relationship with her."

"Your past relationship."

"What'd I say?"

Tessa leaned against the ladder. "Nick, are you certain you're over Madelyn? Because if you're not, things could get really rough with you working here."

"Excuse me."

Nick and Tessa glanced to the open doorway where Maddie now stood. Any fleeting hope he might have had that she hadn't overheard Tessa's comment was squashed by the tightness in her jaw and the squint around her eyes. She was dressed in a dark pink workout suit that looked great with her coloring. She hadn't been wearing the casual clothes this morning.

Nick rolled to his feet. "Hi, Maddie."

He pulled Tessa up. Maddie's eyes focused on their clasped hands.

"Madelyn Walsh, this is Tessa Logan. My brother's wife."

A polite smile. The women shook hands. "Hi, Tessa."

There was no *I've heard about you. Nick talked to me about contacting you, reuniting with his family. I urged him to do it.*

Instead, Maddie gestured to the room. "Looks terrific in here. I like the color."

Tessa jabbed his ribs. "See, I told you."

"It's nice of you to come to help, Tessa. I offered to get some volunteers in to do this for him, but he wanted to do it by himself. His usual M.O."

"He isn't painting alone. My family will be here to pitch in—" she checked her watch "—anytime. I hope you get to meet them."

"I'm sorry, I probably won't. I'm leaving soon. I have a yoga class at six." She tugged on her top's drawstring. "Hence the suit."

She was taking yoga? And cooking classes?

"Yoga?" Tessa's face brightened. "I've been planning to find a studio. Would you recommend yours?"

"Yes. It's the best yoga center in Rockford. I'll pick up a brochure for you and give it to Nick." To him, she said, "I stopped in to tell you that I have bad news. The funding for a second counselor to help you run the group was denied. We've got a call into Albany, where the money was supposed to come from, but John doesn't hold out much hope."

Tessa and Nick exchanged glances.

"That's unfortunate. Tessa was just telling me what a good idea it was."

"Yes, I heard Tessa and you talking."

Nick shifted uncomfortably.

"In any case, I'm not giving up. We'll have someone by tomorrow afternoon even if I have to assign another staff member."

"Seems to me everybody's already overextended."

"Schedules are full, yes. I'll keep you informed." She pointed to the walls. "Again, this looks great. Tessa, nice to meet you."

Maddie had just started away when two whirlwinds burst through the door. They collided with her, and she stumbled backward. Nick grabbed her by the arms.

Amidst the screeches of his nieces'—"Sorry…" and "Oh, no…" and his brother's deep, "Girls…uh-oh…"—Nick was aware of only one thing.

Maddie close to him again. Her upper arms were solid, supple. The shampoo she used smelled like lilacs. Her hair brushed his cheek, its texture still silky.

She recovered before he did. Wrenching out of his grasp, she righted herself.

"I'm sorry." Dan drew one of his daughters close. "My kids were anxious to see their uncle. This is Sara." He patted the other's head. "And this is Molly."

"Hello. I'm Madelyn Walsh."

Dan's eyebrows skyrocketed and he threw Nick a questioning look. Nick shrugged.

"Did we hurt you?" Molly asked.

"Um…no, no, I'm fine."

Nick cleared his throat. "Sorry. The girls are overexuberant."

Breaking away from Dan, Sara approached Maddie and stood before her. "Sorry, ma'am."

She smiled at his niece, a genuine, pure-Maddie smile that had often been directed at him in the past.

Nick was mesmerized by it. "Don't worry, honey, no harm done."

Not to her, maybe. After holding her, even briefly, Nick knew he would spend another night tearing the covers off the bed. *Any* physical contact with this woman was going to ruin his peace of mind.

Tessa came forward. "Madelyn, this is my husband, Dan."

"Nice to meet you." Maddie nodded to his family. "All of you." She'd never met them before because Nick had been estranged from Dan when he and Maddie were together.

Dan kept a poker face, but Nick could guess what he was thinking. "You, too."

"Nice to bump into you," Molly said, chuckling.

Maddie gave a short laugh and the tension eased. "If you'll excuse me. Nick, I'll get back to you on the grant."

Nick watched her leave. When he turned around, he caught sight of Dan's face. "What?" he asked.

THE YOGA INSTRUCTOR, Hillary, sat in the middle of the wooden floor in lotus position. Early March meant the days turned dark at 6:00 p.m., and the inside of the cavernous loft of Open Heart Yoga was in shadows. "Keep your eyes closed," Hillary said softly, "chin down, sternum up, tailbone settling into the floor or bolster."

As Madelyn had only taken classes for two years,

she was elevated on a cushion, her legs merely crossed, not sliding easily into a complete lotus. Beside her, Bethany Hunter, who'd been at this since she was twenty, was in perfect harmony with the instructor.

Blank your mind. Don't think. Concentrate on the light. Breathe in. Out.

Still, no harmony. Damn it! Damn him!

"Madelyn, ease the tension in your shoulders. Get rid of that frown."

Chastised by the instructor, Madelyn tried like hell to relax.

For an hour and a half.

It never happened.

When the final *namaste* came, Madelyn's stomach was still in knots.

"That felt terrific," Beth said, stretching out her legs and wiggling her toes.

"Yeah, terrific."

Her friend nodded to the huge statue on the front altar. "Buddha will smite you for lying in his sanctuary."

"I know somebody else he can smite instead."

Beth stood. She was a tall, graceful woman with a slender body and a core of inner strength. "Come on, let's put our props away and go get juice."

When they were settled into a corner of the juice bar downstairs, Beth sipped her cranberry drink. "It didn't go so well with Nick?"

"On how many levels do you want to hear about it?"

"All of them." She squeezed Madelyn's hand. "I wish I'd been at work the last two days."

"You had your own problems, Beth." She took a swig of her drink, enjoying the tart pineapple flavor. "It was hard to see him."

"I'll bet that's an understatement. How'd he react to the news about Lucy? And you?"

"He was shocked." She tried hard not to feel sorry for him. She had to stifle all emotional involvement with this man, or the floodgates would open.

"Still think you can work with him?" When John had asked her to come back and then told her Nick was also returning, she and Beth had discussed the issue at length. Beth had advised against it.

"Yep. I can. For John and for the Center."

"Tell me about the meeting."

"Right off the bat, he objected to the schedule sheets. Then he balked at the idea of running his program by me."

"Nick doesn't deal well with authority." Beth smiled. "It's one of the reasons he understands kids so well."

"He tried to talk me out of a second counselor for his group sessions and absolutely refuses to participate in the staff support group."

"I warned you about the last thing. But objecting to the additional counselor is bad judgment. And I'm kind of surprised. He usually sees what's best for kids."

"Well, we ambushed the hell out of him with my being his boss."

To be fair, Madelyn also told Beth about the space he'd set up for the teens. However, she didn't mention that while he'd been painting the room, he'd been talking to his lovely sister-in-law about *her* or that, when his nieces had unbalanced Madelyn, Nick had grabbed on to her. That slight touch had brought back so many associations. At that moment, she'd realized she couldn't afford to get anywhere near him physically. She'd have to keep her distance—a lot like an alcoholic had to stay away from booze.

"Always the innovator. That's the Nick Logan I know and love."

Madelyn clenched her hands in her lap.

Insightful, and closer to Madelyn than any other human being, Beth watched her friend for a minute. "Maddie, I know you hated that I talked to him after he left you and had an e-mail correspondence with him, but A, I'm a minister and I can't turn away people in need. And B, he suffered. Almost as much as you did."

Madelyn drew in a breath that would make Hillary proud and released it slowly. "I realize all that. And I'm glad you were there for him. He got cold feet and ditched me but I was still in love with him."

"He ditched you because he was in love with you, too. In his words, he 'couldn't handle how his life had begun to revolve around you.'"

She shook her head. "You don't leave someone because you love them too much." She arched a brow. "And I bet he never used the *L*-word to you. I know he didn't to me. It's not in his vocabulary." Of course, Madelyn had held back that particular declaration, too.

A silence. "Isn't that a little unfair? You know what caused his commitment issues." Beth hesitated. "You knew it when you got involved with him."

After Daniel Logan Sr. had embezzled a half million dollars out of the bank he worked at and gone to jail for it, Nick had rebelled. Because she couldn't handle him, his mother had kicked Nick out of her house when he was sixteen. A "tough love" kind of thing that had backfired in ways Claire Logan couldn't have imagined.

Still what Nick had done to Maddie was unforgivable. "At some point, you have to stop blaming your past for your present insecurities and faults and take control of your life."

Across the table, Beth gave her an indulgent smile. "You're so strong, Maddie. Not everybody could overcome what you did."

Madelyn shivered, remembering her absent father, her alcoholic mother and how she'd practically supported herself since she was eleven. For most of her early life, she'd been intimately acquainted with the word *impoverished*.

"Because you overcame such odds, you think everybody else can, too."

"Maybe. But, Beth, he's a psychotherapist, he should be able to figure out a way to deal with his personal issues."

Beth laughed. "If that were true, I'd be able to forgive my ex for all the damage he's done. I'm a minister, but truthfully, when he disappoints Parker, I want to kill the S.O.B."

Madelyn loved Bethany like a sister and didn't want to fight with her, especially over Nick. "Let's stop talking about Nick. I can't change the things that happened in the past. I can just try to work with him at the Center."

"What are you going to do about the additional counselor?"

"No money for one. But I'm not going to let a little thing like that violate my new policy."

"Can you assign Reid to help?"

"No. He's taking a vacation—long overdue. There's something going on in his family he won't talk about, but I gather this time away is important."

"John can't do it."

"No, it would be too much of a burden now."

"I'd help out but I can't afford any more time out of the house. Parker needs me there."

"I wouldn't let you anyway. You already put in more hours than the local ministerium pays you for." Beth was a part-time pastor at a local church, and her part-time salary at the Center was footed by a group of inner-city churches. "How is Parker?"

"Better." Beth scowled. "I'm so mad at his father.

He canceled their plans on Sunday, which sent my son into a serious depression."

"I'm mad at him, too."

They chuckled, as if being angry at the men in their pasts would help.

Beth studied Madelyn with what Madelyn called her *minister look*. "You aren't thinking about doing the counseling yourself, are you Maddie?"

She didn't say anything.

"That would be a very bad decision."

"I know." Her throat tightened at the mere thought. "And I swear to God, I don't want to work that closely with Nick."

"We'll find another way."

"By three o'clock tomorrow?"

"Hey, God does some of Her best work on deadline."

Madelyn laughed, and so did Beth. Once again, Madelyn was grateful to have this woman in her life.

She had a lot to be grateful for. Friends like Beth and John. A job she loved. Enough material things.

Hearing a thud from above where another yoga session had started, she vowed not to let Nick Logan ruin one more class, one more hour, one more minute of her good and happy life.

"WHAT ARE YOU still doing here?"

Nick turned to find John in the doorway of the newly painted group session room. "Is it that late?"

"Eight o'clock."

"I wanted to finish up as much as I could tonight."

He scanned the area. "Not too shabby for one day's work, is it?"

John wandered inside. "Who paid for these?" He swiped his hand over a beanbag chair, one of a set of four. "And the futon? And the director's chairs?"

He missed the table and "kewl" lamps, as Nick's nieces had called them.

"Everything was cheap. I got it all at the furniture warehouse outlet."

"How much?"

"Two fifty."

"Did Maddie approve the expense?"

"What? Without bloodletting? No, I paid for it myself so I didn't have to open a vein."

"I thought so." John slouched down into a beanbag. "Ouch. Wow, I'm getting old."

"Try the futon."

When John was settled on the couch, he looked up at Nick. "You can't spend your own money on this place."

Though social work didn't pay big bucks, Nick lived frugally and had saved some money. "I don't have anybody else to spend it on, except maybe my nieces."

"Whose fault is that?"

Nick stared down at the man who was more of a father to him than his own had been. A friend Nick had almost lost because of what he'd done to Maddie.

She's like a daughter to me and Lucy. You're like a son. What the hell are you doing to your lives?

Nick's response had been so weak, so milquetoast, he'd been embarrassed by it. *John, when she thought she was pregnant, I began to realize what I'd gotten myself into. I wouldn't be any good at that kind of life. I'd be like Daniel. Claire was right, I have his genes. Maddie's better off without me.*

John had practically begged. *Please, Nick, don't do this.*

"Where are you, son?"

"Thinking about the past." He glanced up at the ceiling fan Dan had put in. "I…" Damn it, he *had* learned something in the last three years. "About how grateful I am that you didn't write me off after what I did to her."

"Never gonna happen." The expression on John's face was full of warmth and acceptance. "No matter how hard you try to alienate everybody who cares about you."

Nick dropped down into a director's chair opposite him. "John, I've agreed to stay on. But I hope Maddie doesn't get hurt in the process."

"She tells me she won't. Otherwise, I wouldn't have hired her back." John smoothed his hand over the light wood arm of the futon. "She's moved on, Nick. She had a steady guy in her life for almost a year."

"Joe?" The macho paramedic who'd dated Maddie before Nick.

"No, somebody else. Somebody serious."

Did the lights dim? "Who?"

"A nice guy. Professor at the University of Rockford where she did her doctoral work. Lucy and I spent some time with them."

"Huh!" His stomach roiled. "Well, I'm glad for her."

"You should be. He worshipped the ground she walked on."

"You talk in the past tense. What happened?"

"He got a job at American University in D.C. before Maddie came back to the Center. He wanted her to go to Washington with him."

Couldn't be she cared about him enough if she'd passed on that. "Why didn't she?"

"I'm not sure."

John waited a beat. "What about you? Any women in your life?"

"No. There was someone, but…"

She was married. Still, his relationship with Katie Gardner had been comfortable and easy. Probably because there was no danger of commitment. She'd loved her husband, but he was absent and neglectful. They'd even separated a time or two, though they always got back together again.

"But what?" John asked.

Because he was embarrassed by the affair, Nick couldn't tell his friend the truth. "It didn't work out. End of story."

"All right. But I'm here if you need to talk about it."

"Sure."

"And do me a favor? Be careful with Maddie. Don't oppose her on everything."

"I— You're right. This has all been a shock to me. And I was blindsided by the changes around here."

"They're solid ones."

"Maybe. I don't know how I'm going to manage that support group thing. The thought of spilling my guts in front of people I don't know well, especially my colleagues, makes me crazy." He sighed. "And, yes, I do get the irony. I ask clients to do exactly that. It's the old 'physician heal thyself' cliché."

John chuckled. "You're not alone. A lot of mental-health workers find opening up difficult. The first time I talked about Zoe and what her death did to mine and Lucy's marriage, I broke down."

"I'm sorry you had to go through that."

"So, young man, if I can put it out there, you can, too." He stood. "Now grab your car keys."

"Why? I want to make some informational posters to put up on the walls temporarily."

"Not now. Our church members are still bringing us food every week and there's a spaghetti dinner waiting as we speak. Lucy would hit the roof if she knew I'd left you working here. You're coming home with me."

"Like the prodigal son?"

His friend's face sobered. "Nick, why do you continue to see yourself like that?"

"Like what?"

"You know." He nodded to the door. "And in case you don't, Lucy will fill you in while she stuffs you with pasta."

CHAPTER THREE

NICK STARED at the eight young faces in the room and felt a surge of adrenaline rush though him. "Hi, everybody. Thanks for getting here on time."

Some of the kids said hello. A couple watched him with suspicious eyes. A boy in a beanbag chair, which he'd dragged to a far corner, was reading the posters Nick had tacked onto the wall. Another, in a wheelchair, doodled in a notebook on his lap. A girl, who'd taken the futon, appeared to be text messaging on her cell phone.

The door behind him opened before he could continue, and Nick sighed. It must be the new counselor. Though Maddie hadn't mentioned a name, she'd assured him someone would be here. This morning they'd had a row about his paying for the furniture and he hadn't seen her since. He pasted on a phony smile and glanced over his shoulder.

"Hi, sorry I'm late."

"Hi, Madelyn." He cocked his head. "What do you mean, you're late?"

"I'm your second counselor."

Like hell. On Monday, he'd wondered how this

situation could get any worse. Now he knew. He'd had a bad enough time being around her for the three days he'd been back at the Center. There was no way he was going to share counseling duties with her.

She smiled at the kids. "Hello, everyone."

Nick was about to ask to speak to her in the hall when he noticed the expression on the face of one of the girls. She'd yet to take a seat and had been wandering around the room as if she was going to bolt. When she saw Maddie, the stiffness seemed to leave her body. "Dr. Walsh, hi."

Maddie walked over to the girl. "Hi, Kara." She sat in a director's chair and Kara followed suit in one close by.

Nick gave them a weak smile. "Obviously, I'm surprised we have another counselor. But glad for the help. Welcome, Madelyn."

She nodded.

Stretching his legs, Nick addressed the group. "So, here we are." He pointed to the food he'd set out on a low table—chips, cookies and some fruit. "Help yourself to snacks first and there's soda in the fridge by the door. I'll give you a few minutes to get what you want before we start."

When the kids began to mill about, he stood and crossed the room. Kara had gone to get a soda, so he took her chair and leaned in close to Maddie. "What the hell do you think you're doing?"

The red tunic and pants she wore darkened the color of her eyes. "Just what I said."

"Maddie, no. This is a bad idea."

"It's the only idea." Her jaw tightened. "Do you think I'd be here if it weren't?"

"Why didn't you warn me?"

"This isn't the time to get into that, Nick."

When he saw the kids returning to their seats, he stood. "We'll talk later. I want some answers." Back in their midst, he took a sip from the bottle of water he'd put by his chair. Its cool wetness didn't soothe the heat in his throat. With a poise he didn't feel, he started his intro. "What I'd like to do today is get to know you better and hopefully have you get to know each other some." Actually, he'd memorized the contents of their folders and would only have to refer to the clipboard by his side in an emergency. "Then I'd like to talk about how our group will run. You all are going to decide much of how we'll operate here."

A snort from the corner. He glanced at the kid's name tag. "What, Hector?"

"Real choices, dude, or phony ones like they give us in the group home?"

Hector Santos and his twin sister Carla had been placed in a teen shelter after their father had brutally beaten and killed their mother—in front of both sixteen-year-olds. The elder Santos had been put in jail, with no bail, and the kids were going to have to testify in court about what they'd seen. Meanwhile, they were headed to foster care.

"I hope I give you real choices. But if I don't, you

got the job of telling me I'm not living up to what I said I'd do."

The kid shrugged.

"Remember, Hector—and all of you—I'm fully aware that you're the victims of crimes, and not the perpetrators. Nor are you at-risk juvenile delinquents. This is *your* group. Together, we have to find the best ways to help you deal with any issues caused by your victimization."

Most of the kids nodded or made eye contact at his acknowledgment of their status.

"Let's start with introductions." He patted his chest near the square that held his name. "I'm Nick Logan. I have a bachelor's degree in social work and a masters in psychology, but more important, I've worked with teenagers extensively in the past." He held up a sheet. "On here, along with other information, are the e-mail addresses of three kids from my last job who've agreed to tell you what kind of guy I am."

That brought surprise to many of their faces.

"What do we call you?" A skinny boy with red hair that looked like he'd chopped it himself asked the question. J. J. Camp. Before his fifteenth birthday, J. J. Camp had fallen victim to a series of tragic incidents. His parents had been killed in a car accident a year ago and he'd gone to live with his aunt in the city. As the new kid on the block, and a gawky one to boot, tough inner-city school life had been miserable for him. He'd consistently been the brunt of bullying. Two of his taunters had been suspended for a month and sent to juvenile detention because, in one of their harassment incidents, J.J.'s arm had been broken. It was still in a cast. Nick suspected the bullying hadn't ended there. One set of bullies had just been replaced by another.

"I hope you'll call me good things, J.J.," Nick joked.

"I mean, Dr. Logan, Mr. Logan, Nick?"

"Either of the last two. Though I'd prefer Nick."

"What about you?" Hector's sister Carla asked Maddie. The twins shared the same dark curly hair and big, almost-black eyes. "When we met that day we signed up, we called you Dr. Walsh."

"That or Madelyn's fine, Carla." Maddie's smile was forced. Too bad. If she'd let Nick know she'd be joining them, he and she could have discussed how she wanted to be addressed.

"Now that that's settled, let me tell you about the schedule." He was giving them time to acclimate before he asked them to introduce themselves. He held up the paper again. "The schedule for the group sessions is on here; we'll meet in this room. I'm offering them Tuesday after school, Thursday nights and Saturday mornings."

Hector shook his head. "I gotta work on Saturday."

His sister said, "And I got softball practice most days at three."

"That's why there are three sessions. I'm trying to make this easy on you. You're welcome to come to all of them, but I do want a firm commitment from you that you'll attend at least two. This support group isn't meant to be a drop-in thing." Since they'd all agreed to come—either by choice or coercion from their guardians or parents—he expected their cooperation. "For individual counseling appointments, we can meet here at the Center, at your school if we can find some place inconspicuous or even at a coffee shop. I hear the Spot is still hopping in Rockford."

From the corner of his eye, he saw Maddie shift in her seat. One of the differences in their style was his informality. She played by the rules . In the past, he'd liked to tease her out of that box.

Kara leaned over and her light brown hair obscured her face as she whispered something to Maddie, who responded to her privately, then said aloud, "I won't be doing any individual counseling with you. But I promise to be at all these group sessions. And as Nick told you, he's very experienced."

Nick rose and picked up one of the brand-new notebooks. "First off, I'm suggesting we write in these at each session. If the activity doesn't work for us, we can stop, but I'd like to try this because it *has* worked with kids in the past. The entry today should be one you can share with us."

Anne Nguyen raised her hand and Nick nodded for her to ask her question. A fourteen-year-old Asian girl, she'd been traumatized by a break-in at her house. Her father had been severely injured when he'd tried to stop the intruder, who'd been caught, tried and put behind bars. "What about other entries?"

"I thought we'd have several types." He moved to

the whiteboard he'd set up. "One will be a communication between you and us." He wrote down, *types of journals,* then *you, Nick and Madelyn.* "Or you can choose one of us to read it. The second will be for *teen eyes only.*"

"Sounds like a song." From his wheelchair, Tommy Danzer looked up for the first time. His curly blond hair fell over big and distrusting blue eyes. The victim of a drive-by shooting, the boy had a spinal cord injury and would never recover. He was only fifteen years old.

"Yeah, but don't expect me to sing. I'd only do that to punish you." Nick smiled. "Some entries you can record and *plan to share* at a later date."

Slouched in a chair far away from the group, Nato Keyes called out, "Yo, man. I don't do writing." The young black boy had been assaulted on the street and his assailant was awaiting arraignment. In the intake notes, Madelyn had indicated his anger seemed to be seething inside him. Nick hoped to bring it to the surface.

Nick picked up a different notebook from the stack and brought it to Nato. "I happen to have a journal without lines." He also knew from the intake interview Nato was an artist. "You can draw or doodle entries. But you have to discuss some of them."

"No shit?"

"Speaking of that, I'd prefer we keep the language clean in here. Even if it's not your or my style." He hoped including himself would ease the caveat.

"What about language in the journals?" Hector asked.

Since she needed to be included, Nick looked to Maddie. She said, "Anything's fine by me in the journal, but I'd prefer you didn't read aloud language that might make somebody else uncomfortable."

"Can you guys live with that?" Nick asked.

"What if we can't?" Hector's mutinous expression was one Nick was familiar with. When he was the boy's age, he'd perfected it.

"Por favor, el hermano," Carla said softly.

So Hector was here for his sister. She might be his Achilles' heel and Nick's entry into his life.

Hector shrugged. *"Sí, bien."*

Nick made eye contact with everybody but Kara, who wouldn't look at him. Her file stated that she'd been beaten up by some girls in the school parking lot, but Madelyn had commented in her folder that something about her story didn't ring quite true. Counselors paid attention to gut instincts.

Maddie asked, "Kara, this okay with you?"

"I guess."

"Shamika?" Nick addressed the one girl who hadn't yet spoken and was still fiddling with her cell phone. Overweight, with cornrows gracing her dark head, she was quiet, reports said. Which might explain why she spent most of her time on the computer and had become the victim of an online predator. He'd ended up being a level-three sex offender and had taken her halfway across the country before he was apprehended. He was back in jail now, as Shamika was under seventeen, the legal age of consent in New York.

Her face was impassive. "Yeah, no worries."

"First entry, then. Write down what you'd like to get out of this group. Why you're here. Anything specific you might want to do. You can read all or parts of it today to us. Any portion can be marked private, which means neither Madelyn nor I will read it. But you've got to share at least one thing. Also, put in what snacks you want to have this week." He glanced at the clock. "Ten minutes. Madelyn and I will write, too, of course. We'll never ask you to do something we wouldn't do."

"That's a switch," J.J. said.

"Not for me. It's the way I operate." Nick passed around the books. "I hope you'll come to see that."

"What about you, Dr. Walsh?" Tommy asked. "You gonna do what you ask us to?"

"Yes. I fully agree with everything Nick has said."

Hmm. Now that *was* a switch.

J.J. WROTE FURIOUSLY in his journal.

Duh!! Like hell this is gonna be our group. Adults always say crap they don't mean, like those assholes at school. My aunt's okay, even though she looks at me like I walked off some Martian space craft. This guy'll probably be like the ones at school. We'll play some freaking games for a while, then he'll make us do whatever he wants. The chick, too. She seemed cool at the intake interview, but that didn't mean anything.

J.J. glanced up and saw the other kids writing. He looked at the posters on the wall. They were printed from the computer. The first showed statistics on teen victimization. It read:

Teens are twice as likely as adults to become victims of crimes.

58 per thousand of 16- to 19-year-olds are victimized.

46 per thousand of 12- to 15-year-olds.

Revictimization is 80% for teens who've been victimized once.

Right on, man. Nobody knew the number of times he'd been stuffed into lockers. Knocked against the wall. Doused with soda or water or whatever the frigging jocks had handy. Cripes, a couple of girls had even gotten into the act. His arm hurt like hell today, though the doc said it was healing. He wished his father were still alive. He could have helped. He was such a great guy… Even his mother would have been there for him. Now they were in long, cold graves. Sometimes J.J. wished he'd been with them on that rainy night when they'd skidded into a guardrail. He'd never even had a chance to say goodbye.

When the hole inside him threatened to gobble him up, he went back to the journal.

> Anyway, what do I want from this place? How about pizza and beer for snacks? How about somebody to believe me? How about other kids who don't look at me like I'm a weirdo?

He felt his eyes well with the dreaded moisture. Damn it, why had he let his aunt convince him to come here?

Because he was afraid she'd turn on him if he didn't. Because he couldn't stand how much he hurt inside and couldn't handle the anger that never seemed to go away. These people might not be able to help, but they couldn't make his life worse.

It couldn't get any worse.

MADELYN FINISHED her journal entry about what she wanted to happen in this group. It wasn't much different from what Nick had proposed, though she would have preferred the kids refer to her by her formal title. And she wouldn't have thought to meet with them at a coffee shop.

"Time's up." Nick's voice was clear and strong and confident. It even made her feel safe, and she knew better than to buy into his coaxing ways. "Let's share some of our thoughts. Anybody want to start?"

No takers.

Madelyn jumped in. "I will." She read from her first page. "I'd like to decorate the journal covers next time with something that reflects our personalities. Who we are. And I think we should do some ice-breakers then, too, to get us warmed up to talking about our feelings. I hope everybody will participate because that's the only way to help each other. However, my vote is for a pass system, where we don't have to share if we don't want to."

"That's chunk," Nato said. Madelyn had recently learned that *chunk* indicated approval.

Hector added, *"Sí, Señora."*

Madelyn smiled at them. "But, guys, I don't think we should be able to pass all the time."

"I agree with that." She looked over to see Nick had gone to the whiteboard again and had written down what she'd suggested.

Madelyn held up her journal. "The rest is for my eyes only." She'd written about how difficult it was to be here with Nick.

"Did you do that?" Kara asked. "Write private stuff?"

"Yes." She angled her head at the girl. "Kara, you know, adults don't have it all together. We have issues."

Nick stared at Madelyn. "We mess things up. We make bad decisions."

"I guess I know that," Kara said.

"Let's go on." Nick scanned the kids. "One of you want to start?"

Again, Anne Nguyen raised her hand.

"You can just speak out, Anne," Nick told her.

"I want this all to be private from our parents."

Nick wrote *privacy* on the board, then set down the marker. Sticking his hands in the pockets of his jeans, he leaned back on his heels. "I think your request is a key here. But I have to tell you some parameters. You can share feelings that you don't want your parents to know about. But if either Madelyn or I sense you're going to harm yourself or someone else, we can't and won't keep that private."

"Will you tell Dr. Walsh what we talk about in private sessions?" Tommy asked.

"I'm going to ask for your permission for that," Madelyn answered before Nick could. "I can help you better in these group sessions if I know what you and Nick talked about."

Tommy's expression was challenging. "You promise it won't go further?"

"I do." She looked at Nick.

He said, "You have my word."

Madelyn struggled with that....

Maddie, please, I need to touch you, hold you. You have my word, I won't hurt you, emotionally or physically....

"Madelyn, Carla asked you a question."

"I'm sorry, what?"

"You're head of this place?"

"Yes, I am."

"Can you keep that promise?"

"I haven't broken one yet." She shot a pointed look at Nick.

He cleared his throat. "It's settled then, if no one else has an opinion on the privacy."

Most of them nodded.

"Nato? You go next."

The boy shrugged as if he didn't care about any of this. "I want pretzels and Dr Pepper."

The corners of Nick's mouth turned up. "I'll go grocery shopping. What else?"

The kid held his gaze unflinchingly. "I pass."

"Hector?" Nick asked.

"Burritos and fried rice."

"That might have to wait until a dinner gathering."

As Maddie listened to everybody else, she wondered how Nick was going to go about reaching the boys who were showing signs of resistance. He was a skilled counselor, but some kids did fall through the cracks.

Like he had. When she began to think about his difficult adolescence, she stopped short. Damn it, she wasn't going to feel sorry for him.

KARA GLANCED around the room. After they'd introduced themselves, Nick had given them one last assignment. Write about how they were feeling at the end of the session.

On the wall was a poster of common reactions to victimization. He said they could write those feelings down if they applied and go from there.

So she wrote, "Isolated, helpless, powerless." She bit her lip. "Shy. Don't like the boys in the group. Glad Dr. Walsh is here. Wonder if I'm ever going to get better."

Someone touched her arm. "Kara, are you all right?"

She looked up at Dr. Walsh. "Huh?"

"You're crying."

Her hands went to her face. "Oh, God."

Dr. Walsh stood. "Come on, let's go outside for a minute."

She couldn't get her breath.

"It's okay, Kara. It's okay."

She managed to stand. Nick nodded to Dr. Walsh, who led her out and down to the ladies' room. Inside, she wet some paper towels and gave them to Kara. When Kara just held on to them, Dr. Walsh took them back and pressed them to Kara's face, which felt like it was burning up. "Better?"

"Uh-huh. I'm sorry. I hate being such a tweaker."

"Never apologize for your reactions in there, Kara. You're going to see a lot of the kids breaking down."

"Yeah, I'll bet Nato and Hector are real criers."

Dr. Walsh chuckled, then got serious. "They'll show it in other ways."

"By giving Nick a hard time."

"He can hold his own."

"I'm glad you're in the group."

"Then so am I."

Kara wished she could meet with Dr. Walsh individually and not Nick, but she was afraid to ask.

Instead, she pushed away from the sink. "I'm better now. Do I have to go back in?"

"You don't have to do anything. But it might help you feel more comfortable next time if you faced everybody now."

"I guess." She hesitated. "I don't think I'm gonna make it here."

Dr. Walsh squeezed her shoulder. "Don't be so quick to judge. Give us a fair shot."

"Okay." She would. Even though she knew neither Nick nor Dr. Walsh could understand what she was going through.

When she'd come home with visible bruises, Kara had told her folks she'd been beaten up in the school parking lot by a bunch of girls she couldn't identify. It was a lie. She couldn't tell anybody the truth. Ever. Her parents had made her come to the RCVC, and she didn't fight it because she was afraid, if she did, somehow they'd find out what really happened, and she couldn't let anybody know that.

Because what had happened was all her fault.

NICK SMILED and spoke to each teen as they left, even Nato and Hector, who grunted, "Later, bro," as they headed out. Then he crossed to the door and closed it.

"That went well, don't you think?"

Count to ten. Twenty. Now, turn around. "No thanks to you." His voice was deadly calm, which was how it got when he was angry. *This* was too much to expect of him, and he was going to tell her so. Because he was around her again, he hadn't been sleeping well, or eating or anything! The idea of working in this group with her was outrageous.

"Excuse me? I thought I contributed pretty well."

"Tell me the real reason you did something as unprofessional as volunteering to be the second counselor and then springing it on me in front of all these kids? You of all people know how important first impressions are with crime victims."

"You were great with them."

"Answer the question."

"I already told you I couldn't find anybody else."

"Why didn't you warn me?"

She raised her chin. "I knew you'd object. And try to find a way to keep me out. I couldn't let that happen."

"When did you get so underhanded? You used to be an open book."

"It wasn't underhanded. It was expedient. I would have won in the end, anyway."

"Of course, because you run the place." He threaded a hand through his hair. "Why the hell did we think we could do this? Work together?"

Her faced reddened. "I know where *my* head's at. Under no circumstances am I going to let you run my life any longer."

"Any longer? What does that mean?"

"Nothing."

"Tell me."

"Back off, Nick."

Maybe he should. "Maddie, this isn't going to work. We can't be together for…what—" he glanced at the clock "—a few minutes without arguing."

Pivoting to face the chair, she picked up her journal. "You'll have to do something about that then."

He grabbed her arm and whirled her around. "I can't work so closely with you. How many different ways can I say that?"

He expected retreat. Instead, she stepped toward him. "Get over it, Nick. Rule number one around here is we do what's best for kids. My being in the group is good, if for no other reason than I was there to take care of Kara while you finished up with the others. And you know very well some kids react better to women than men and vice versa."

"I can handle them all."

"No, you can't. You're going to have problems with Nato Keyes and Hector Santos."

"Are you criticizing my counseling skills?"

"No. I'm only pointing out why you need the second counselor. Accept the idea that you're not playing this alone."

"Fine, I'll accept another counselor. Just not you."

"There's no other choice! For God's sake, don't you think I'd have jumped at it if there was? I tried to get someone else and couldn't. We're in this together, no matter how much you dislike it."

"Do you like it?"

"Are you *kidding?*" She looked horrified. "I hate

it. I hope that's some consolation." She circled around him and reached the door before he stopped her with his words.

"It's not, Maddie. It's no consolation at all."

Her back still to him, she said, "You'll have to find a way to deal with it. So will I."

And then she was gone.

CHAPTER FOUR

"THIS IS SO SWEET of you, Nick." Lucy Kramer's brown eyes sparkled in the sun shining down through the glass roof of the entrance to the Blue Cross Arena. "We love to come to the Amerks games, but parking is horrible. John hates to drive down here."

Smiling, Nick leaned over and kissed Lucy's cheek, her comment and her lined skin reminding him of her age. And frailty. "No problem. After I dropped you off here and parked, I only had to walk fifteen blocks back."

"Fifteen blocks!" Her hand went to her heart. "Oh, my."

"Kid-ding. I got a spot two lots over."

Looking less weary today, John chuckled. "He could always get you going, Luce."

Lucy linked arms with Nick. "I don't care. I love having you back in town. We haven't seen nearly enough of you in the last three years." His visits and calls had been regular, but infrequent.

They strolled up to the turnstile. While Nick was parking, John had purchased the admission tickets.

Once they were inside, Nick led the way to their seats. As he got a glimpse of the rink and felt the ever-present chill of the ice, Nick remembered the first time he'd come to one of these games with the Kramers. Who would have guessed the gentle couple would favor a fast-paced, aggressive sport like hockey! Then again, Claire had, too. Dan had played the game in high school—his all-star brother had competed in three varsity sports—and Nick managed to catch some matches in between his bouts of rebellion. His mood darkened when he thought about bringing Maddie to one of these games with the Kramers. She'd worn an Amerks cap and jersey and jeans so tight they'd sent his blood pressure sky-rocketing. She'd rooted loudly for the home team.

"Nick?"

He came out of his daze to see a worried look on John's face. "Sorry, I went off somewhere." He watched the players warm up on the ice. Take practice shots. The crack of the stick on the puck echoed in the wide-open space and the scrape of skates on the ice hurt his teeth.

Casually, Lucy asked, "Are you very angry at us?"

"For what?"

"For how we got you up here?"

"No, of course not. I told you that last week when I came for dinner."

"I know. I've been thinking about it, though. It was a dirty trick. Especially since you don't trust easily."

He put his hand over hers. "Lucy, I'd have come

back to the Center immediately if you'd told me the truth about your circumstances." He had to look away so she wouldn't see the hurt he still felt inside reflected on his face. His voice was surprisingly even when he said, "If I'm angry at anything, it's that you didn't call me when you had the attack."

Lucy teared up. "Thank you, Nick."

"It's water under the bridge. Let's not talk about it anymore."

"I won't. After I ask one more thing. Is it difficult working with Maddie?"

More than words can describe. Again, he kept his voice calm. "It's tense, but we're falling into a routine."

John grunted. "It might've helped if you'd come to the support group yesterday."

"Honestly, John, I'd planned to, but it was the only time I could meet with J. J. Camp. After Thursday's group meeting, I'm sensing he's the most volatile right now. His school counselor worked something out for lunch on Friday."

"Was Maddie angry?"

"Um, some."

You did this on purpose, didn't you?

No, of course not.

I won't have you flouting the rules. Everybody's expected to follow them.

Look, I know I made it clear I didn't want to go to those sessions, but I'm not flouting your rules. I swear what I told you is the truth. I wasn't able to be there.

Her scathing look reminded him that his word was worth nothing to her.

Thankfully, the game began and he watched the big guys fly along the ice, ram into each other and slap shots from one corner to the other, sometimes into the net. One such shot caused John to rise from his seat, stick his fingers in his mouth and whistle. It was good to see him enjoy himself and it reaffirmed Nick's decision to stay at the Center, regardless of the personal havoc working with Madelyn was causing him. At the first period recess, he and John went to get Lucy a Coke and themselves a beer.

As they waited in line, John said, "I have something to ask you."

"Anything."

"I want you to come to the ceremony for the award I'm getting in D.C."

"That would be—" He cut himself off and watched John. "Is Maddie going?"

"Yes."

"Does she know you're inviting me?"

"I told her. She was fine with it."

She was? "Well, sure then, I'll come."

"Great. Now, tell me how the kids are doing."

"Too early to know. They all showed up at Thursday's meeting, but a few missed today's." Maddie had been particularly worried because Kara Sullivan was withdrawn and sullen this morning.

"What are you planning for them?"

Nick discussed some of his ideas. He'd forgotten

what a good sounding board John was; he'd missed the man professionally more than he'd realized. And he'd missed being with both the Kramers, doing normal family-type things that he'd never done with his own parents. Nick had given up a lot besides Maddie when he'd left town.

"Ready for some dinner?" he asked as the game ended. "We could go over to Edibles. You like their artichoke chicken, if I recall, Lucy."

"I'd love to," Lucy said.

There were throngs leaving the game and Nick could see Lucy lagging. He led the older couple to a bench off to the side. "Stay here. I'll go get the car. Watch for it through the window."

John's look was grateful. "Thank you, son."

Outside, the air was warm for the end of March. He'd let the door slam behind him when he saw her, standing on the sidewalk, looking up and down the street, as if she was waiting for someone. Drawing in a deep breath, he stared at the woman who'd given birth to him. Claire Logan was meticulously dressed in a slim green skirt and matching shirt. Her white hair was done up and she wore makeup.

Unfortunately, she spotted him, too. "Oh, Nicolas. Hello."

"Claire."

Her hand tightened on the strap of her purse. "How are you? I haven't seen you since we all moved to Rockford."

After being forced to be civil to her in Orchard

Place so they could both help Dan and Tessa with their problems, he'd intentionally stayed away from her here in Rockford.

"No, you haven't."

Flushed, she appeared surprised at his curt tone.

"If you'll excuse me, I have to get my car."

He was about to step into the street when a Volvo pulled up in front of them; his mother shot a worried glance at it. Nick tracked her gaze and watched a man get out from the front. The guy's gray hair was thinning, but he was tanned and had a spring in his step as he rounded the car.

He halted abruptly. "Nick!"

Despite the lump in his throat, Nick said, "Well, if it isn't dear old Dad."

CURSING HIMSELF for overreacting, Nick jogged to his car with demons on his heels. Having faced Claire for the first time in months and Daniel for the first time in twenty years, the analogy was appropriate.

Nick found his rented sedan—his Eclipse was in the shop, but should be fixed any day now—and fished in his jeans pocket for the keys. He dropped them to the ground. Cursing, he knelt down to pull them from under the vehicle. When he stood, he saw the Volvo drive up and block him in.

How dare they?

Leaning against the car, squelching any sign of being affected, he waited. Both Claire and Daniel got out.

"What do you want?" he asked.

Up close, he noted the wrinkles in Daniel's face and that his eyes were cloudy. The man had aged. Prison would do that to you. The blood began to pound in Nick's head as an image of the other kids' taunts slammed into him: *Your father's a convict... Hey, you think somebody in prison already made him their bride... You're a troublemaker, just like him.* Suddenly Nick was in high school again, confused, embarrassed and scared out of his mind.

"I want to talk to you," Daniel said, breaking the spell and making Nick realize where he was.

Claire was staring at him with a wounded expression. As if she'd been the one who'd been hurt. She said, "Nicolas..." and he was once again catapulted into the past....

I've had it, Nicolas. You are to leave my house immediately.

Mom, please, I'm sorry. I'll be good. I promise.

I can't do this anymore. You have to go.

Give me another chance.

You were there when the counselor said one more time. This is it. Pack your bags.

Nick couldn't remember packing his bags or leaving the only home he'd ever known. But what had never left him, what burned inside him like acid, was the gut-wrenching sense of rejection and the knowledge that he was so unworthy that his own mother wouldn't stand by him. Hell, he'd been sixteen freaking years old.

"I think I've made it perfectly clear I don't want

to talk to you. Either of you." He felt his control slipping, so he retreated further into the protective shell these people had forced him to build.

Daniel nodded at Nick's blocked car. "I'm not leaving till I say my piece."

Glancing at his watch, Nick said, "I have to pick up the older couple I'm with. Even you wouldn't leave them stranded at the arena."

"It'll only take a minute."

"Go ahead then."

Daniel stepped closer to him. Nick breathed deeply, but he'd be damned if he'd retreat.

"I'm sorry I ruined your life, Nick."

Anger now, which was better. "Don't give yourself that much credit. I've got a good life. I just had to straighten out." He shot an angry look at Claire. "All by myself. You did, however, make my adolescence…difficult."

"I'm sorry for that and for all you've suffered and lost because of me."

Daniel had no idea how much Nick had lost. Nick remembered the almost-desperate call Daniel had made to him when he'd been trying to make emotional restitution as per his A.A. requirements. Nick had refused to talk to him. But the reminder of who Nick was had set in motion his breakup with Maddie. A few weeks later, he'd left her.

"Is that all you wanted to say?"

"Not quite. I'm asking for a chance to make amends."

Nick nodded to Claire. "Looks like she's doing enough amending for both of us."

"Nick, please," she said, "We both want a relationship with you."

"Ain't gonna happen, folks."

He told himself the tears in Claire's eyes were crocodile ones. "If you'd let us…we could all go to counseling together."

He angled his head at Daniel. "I have nothing to say to him."

"Then let's, you and I, go see someone."

"I have even less to say to you."

She reached out to his bare arm, where his shirt was rolled up. It was the first time she'd touched him since he was sixteen. He stumbled backward—to get away from her, he told himself.

"I've got to go. At least have the decency not to make the Kramers wait any longer. Lucy had a heart attack a month ago." Then, meanly, he added, "They've been like parents to me, and I want to take care of them."

Claire stepped back as though she'd been slapped.

Daniel said, "It's not over, Nick."

"It was over the day you stole thousands of dollars from Metrobank." His scowled at Claire. "And the day *you* made me leave your precious house so I wouldn't embarrass you anymore."

He managed to open his car door and slide inside. He was sweating so badly, he turned on the engine and put the air-conditioning up high. He gripped the steering wheel to stop his hands from shaking. People—Dan, Maddie, counselors—thought he was overreacting to what had happened to him as a teenager and should be past his resentment by now. Because he'd never told them about the unspeakable things that had happened to him when he'd been abandoned at sixteen to fend for himself. He'd been easy prey for men—and women—on the streets. He'd gotten involved in the drug scene. These people also didn't know that, once he'd learned how to take care of himself, he'd landed in jail before his nineteenth birthday.

He took in big gulps of air, trying to obliterate the obscene memories of those dark years.

In the rearview mirror, he saw Daniel help Claire into his car—a fancy vehicle for an alcoholic ex-con—and drive off. Out of Nick's life.

MADELYN GLANCED at the clock. 8:00 p.m. on a Saturday night. "You need a life," she said, just as her cell phone rang. For a minute she spun a fantasy that it was a husband, urging her to come home, dinner was ready and the kids were waiting for her. Damn it! Where was all this coming from? She punched a button on her cell. "Madelyn Walsh."

"Hi, there, gorgeous." Ted Blake's voice came over the phone, full of warmth and familiarity.

"Ted, nice to hear from you."

"I called, several times. Left messages."

She studied the desk, piled with folders and an overflowing in-box. "I've been swamped."

"Do you miss me?"

"Of course. How's Washington?"

"Lonely."

Uh-oh.

"Don't panic, I'm not pushing you. I heard that John Kramer is getting an award during National Crime Victims' Rights Week here in Washington."

"He is. At the end of the month."

"Will you be coming down for the ceremony?"

"Yes, of course." And so would Nick. She hadn't been shocked that John had asked him, only disappointed. And afraid. Situations kept pushing the two of them together, and she feared the proximity was chipping away at the wall she'd built around herself to keep him out.

"Can we get together when you're here?"

A hesitation. But maybe seeing Ted would be a good thing. She wouldn't have to deal with Nick.

"Please, honey. No strings." Still she didn't agree. "You said you missed me."

"I do." She did. He was the kind of man most women would find attractive. She thought about Nick and how hard it was to be around him. How much his mere presence made her pulse jump, her head hurt. "All right. I'd like to see you, Ted."

"That's what I wanted to hear."

They chatted for a while, and as Madelyn hung up, she heard someone come down the corridor. Their police liaison, Samantha Delaney, was staffing the hotline, so Madelyn wasn't afraid for her physical safety. Besides, the outer door was always locked at night and there was a security guard on the premises. Then she briefly saw Nick before he turned the corner.

So what if he was here? She didn't have to see him. She worked at her desk for a while, and then she came across his memo written after this morning's support group saying he needed to talk to her ASAP, asking her to call his cell. So she punched in the number and got a recording that the service was unavailable. She stood. She'd be damned if she'd stay hiding in her office and keep trying to call him when he was a few feet away. It was unprofessional and stupid.

Sitting at his desk, he had his back to her and was speaking into the landline. "Goddamn it, Dan, did you *know* about this?" He waited. "No, I will not calm down. You could have at least warned me that that f—" he used the *F*-word "—was anywhere near here." A longer pause. "Yeah, I know I told you not to mention him to me and that I refused to see him when he came to Orchard Place." He ran his hand through his hair. "No, no. You're right. Look, I gotta go. I'll call you tomorrow…yeah, me, too." He clicked off. And swore again at the phone.

For a minute, she watched him, his shoulders slumped in the blue-and-white shirt he wore. Then he turned. His navy eyes narrowed on her. "How long have you been there?"

"Long enough."

"You overheard."

"Yes. I take it you saw your father."

"And mommy dearest. Together." She watched his fist curl. "Dan says he's working thirty miles outside of Rockford."

"I'm sorry they're still running your life." She winced. "I didn't mean that the way it came out."

"Of course you did. It's what you accused me of three years ago."

She didn't come farther into the room. "That's over and done, Nick." But she found herself unable to ignore him when he was so obviously shaken. Against her better judgment, she asked, "What happened today?"

"I took John and Lucy to the Amerks game. We bumped into Claire and Daniel. They cornered me in the parking lot and asked to…I don't know…start a new relationship with them or some damn thing. I said no. End of story." He pushed his chair in and, averting his gaze, picked up a pen. "I need to finish up some paperwork for Monday."

"You still haven't dealt with this, have you?"

His head snapped up. "I'm doing fine."

The dismissal angered her. Prompted her to say, "Yeah, you're doing just great."

He glared at her. "My state of mind is none of your business."

She started to turn away but threw out one more salvo. "Do yourself a favor, Nick. Get some counseling."

"I did."

That stopped her.

He leaned back in his chair and looked drained. "Or tried to, anyway." He stared out the window, where darkness had fallen like a curtain. "After you and I split, I went to see a counselor. It didn't help."

Why did that make her heart leap? Softened by the admission, she came into the room and perched on the chair in front of his desk. "How long did you go for?"

"Not long enough, apparently. I couldn't open up. At least not enough."

"You know progress is slow, particularly with a twenty-year grudge."

His look was pained. "Why are we talking about all this?"

She leaned forward. "Because I was just thinking that what I really wanted out of life was a man to care about, a family to go home to." She hesitated. "What about you? Don't you want a family? Someday, with another woman?"

"Maybe someday."

"Then you're going to have to deal with your issues about your parents."

"I told you, my paltry attempt didn't work."

"Is there anyone else you could see? You'll never go on with your life unless you—"

"Hello, there."

Madelyn turned to see Samantha Delaney in the doorway. The twenty-nine-year-old had been added to the staff after Madelyn had left the Center. She was a solid cop and a nice woman. For some reason, Madelyn wondered if Nick would find her short auburn hair and spunky green eyes attractive.

"Sam, hi."

Sam greeted Maddie then looked at Nick. "I'm Samantha Delaney, your friendly police liaison. I also teach a self-defense class for women here at the Center."

"Nick Logan. I wonder if any of my teenage girls would be interested in the self-defense."

"Ask them. I come from a huge family and love kids." She grinned. "So you're Nick Logan. The legend."

Rising, Nick came around the desk and leaned against it. "Yeah, I'm him. But the legend stuff's a stretch."

"Not what I hear."

"From John?"

"No, actually, from other cops in the department. About when you worked in Rockford before."

"Really? I'd like to hear about it someday."

"Hmm." She gave him a very female perusal. "I'd like to tell you someday." She frowned at Madelyn. "What are you guys doing here on a Saturday night? I'm scheduled, but you two aren't."

They spoke at the same time.

"Catching up…"

"Playing catch-up…"

Sam tsked. She was about to say more, when the hotline phone rang. "Gotta go."

"I'm available, if needed," Maddie called after her.

"Me, too," Nick added.

Hotline calls usually just entailed phone counseling or referrals. Periodically, though, someone had to go out. Police. E.M.T.'s. Or one of the on-call staff.

"You guys need a life," Sam said, sing-songing her way out.

As Madelyn watched her go, she thought, *Damn right!* And staying here, talking with Nick wasn't the way to get one. To that end, she said to Nick, "I'm leaving."

"Good idea."

ON MONDAY MORNING, Madelyn and Nick had to work together on the kids' journals. She didn't let her discomfort show as she curled her legs under her and settled into the futon. "I'll take Kara, J.J., Shamika and Nato first. Then we can switch."

Giving her a stack of the books, Nick sat down. He wore black jeans and a gray golf shirt, which showed off his muscles. "What about ours?"

"Excuse me?"

"Are we going to read each other's journals?"

She choked on the coffee she'd taken a sip of. "No. Why would we do that?"

"We said we'd do what the kids did."

"We did. I wrote, you wrote, we can share in the session with them."

She couldn't decipher his expression as he stared at her.

"I don't want to read your journal, Nick. And I certainly don't want you to read mine."

His face colored. "Fine." From his pocket he took out glasses and slid them on. He hadn't worn them three years ago. He looked...different in them. Older. But attractive.

Tearing her gaze away, she picked up the first journal. At her urging, they'd titled their books. And Nick had suggested several modes of expression: poems, dialogue, a series of images, a letter, free writing. For the first time, he'd asked them to tell how they'd been victimized with the intention of sharing with everyone during Tuesday's group session.

Madelyn started with Anne Nguyen's.

Musings by Anne
    Glass shatters, echoing through the entire house. She hears her father swear as he gets up. "Don't go, Papa," she wants to say, but hides her head under the blanket.
    "Call 9-1-1," he says to her mother and then, "I'm going downstairs."
    Across the room, her little sister whimpers. What if something happens to her? "Get in bed with me, Lyn," she whispers.
    Her heart beats fast. Why is Papa going down there? Wait for the police, please!
    Crashes below. Her father yelling. Oh, God, please.
    Sirens.

No sounds down there.

Mama at our door. "Stay here. I'm going down." She holds a baseball bat.

"No, Mama, no."

"Shh."

Loud knocking. "Police. Open up."

A door crashing. "Ma'am." Her mother must be on the staircase.

Whipping out of bed, she runs to it, and sees her father at the landing, bleeding.

POOR ANNE. Objectively, Madelyn knew not to worry about the third person usage in the writing. Victims often recorded the event as if it were happening to someone else. Still, Anne's entry was disturbing. Picking up her pen, Madelyn wrote in the margin. How sorry she was. How frightening that must have been.

At least they'd caught the burglar and he was in jail for a ten-year sentence. Her father was still recuperating.

Kara's was next.

Kara's Journal
Nothing happened, really.
In my head.
Don't make too much of this.
Silly girl.
Just an incident.
I can control this.
No one would understand anyway.
Don't ask, don't tell.

DENIAL WASN'T GOOD. Madelyn suspected Kara knew who her assailants were, but was insisting she didn't, maybe even to herself. She wrote, "Kara, something did happen to you. It's okay to be mad. Scared. Confused. It's okay to want justice. Please, try to admit what happened to you. How you feel." Adding other comforting words, Madelyn spent a little extra time on this one.

Then she went on to J.J.'s.

Jonesing about J.J.

I wanna stuff them in lockers so they choke on their own spit.

Hold them under water in gym class till they suffocate.

Bash their heads in with the baseball bat they carry.

I wanna hear their bones crack, see their blood flow, watch their eyes blur.

AND AT THE END was a section folded and marked private. Madelyn whistled softly.

"What?" Nick asked

"J.J.'s entry is violent."

"Not surprising, with the amount of violence he's experienced. The kids they caught were disciplined, but I think there's still some bullying going on."

"Did he tell you that?"

"No, I sense it. He didn't tell me much in our

session." He sighed. "Of all of them, he worries me the most."

"There's a section marked private."

"Yeah, in one of the journals I skimmed, too."

"It's hard not to read them."

"I know. But we can't."

"Of course." Putting the book on the table, she asked, "Should we worry about the violence in J.J.'s journal?"

"No. I'm glad he's getting it out. Repressing things doesn't help. He needs a release valve. We just have to be vigilant about him. Keep a close eye on those violent tendencies." He went back to reading.

She picked up "SHAMIKA'S HOME PAGE." Oh, damn! "Nick?"

"Hmm?"

"Shamika wrote in computer speak."

He looked up. "Her online life is more real than her actual one, so that fits."

"Thank God they caught that predator." Maddie scanned the entry. "I'm not familiar with all this jargon. I get some of the acronyms, but not all."

Rising, Nick crossed to her and sat down on the futon. "Let me see."

Immediately, she reacted to his nearness. His scent mostly, the same cologne he used to wear. Her throat ached. She moved farther away from him and forced herself to concentrate on the text as she reread it with him.

2DAY IS LIKE 2MORO AND 2NITE. AFAIK
NOTHING WILL CHANGE. BTW, I LIKED HIM.
THOUGHT IT WAS A DATE. IMHO LIFE SUCKS.
LOL THAT YOU THINK YOU CAN HELP. NO1
CAN. OTOH, WHAT ARE MY CHOICES. PLS. SRY.
Y.

NICK TRANSLATED aloud, "Today is like tomorrow
and tonight. As far as I know, nothing will change. By
the way, I liked him. Thought it was a date. In my
humble opinion, life sucks. Laughing out loud that
you think you can help. No one can. On the other
hand, what are my choices? Please. Sorry. Why?"

"How do you know all this?" Madelyn asked.

"I work with teenagers. They love this stuff and
use it in e-mails and text messages to me."

"Do you still keep in touch with kids in Orchard
Place?"

"Yeah. I like to hear from them." He nodded to the
journal. "Adults use these in e-mails, too. Aren't they
in the ones people send you?"

"I only recognize a few. I don't do much personal
e-mailing."

"Ah."

She used to. They'd send each other e-mails and text
messages even though they worked in the same office.
Some were really sexy. She shoved away the thought.
Damn it! This resurrection of memories was exactly
why she shouldn't be working so closely with him.

"How should we respond?"

Nick cocked his head in the way that meant he was thinking. Then a grin spread across his face as he scribbled on the journal. IT WON'T BE EZ SHAMIKA. BUT NETHNG BAD CAN HAPPEN IF YOU OPEN UP 2 US. PROLLY GOOD THINGS. PLS SPK TO US. DON'T W8. WE WAN2 HELP. LET US.

Maddie laughed aloud. "Very clever." She cleared her throat and said what was in her heart. "It's good for the kids that you're here, Nick." Despite how his presence was affecting her, she meant it.

"Yeah?"

She shook her head. "I couldn't do that. You've got a special connection with adolescents, a knack for getting on their level."

"Thanks."

Inordinately pleased by her compliment, Nick picked up another journal from the table.

She stiffened slightly. "Aren't you going back to your chair?"

"Yeah, of course." He stood, disconcerted by her request. "Want to take a break?"

She glanced at her watch. "No. I'm going to lunch with Joe. We need to get these done before then."

"You on friendly terms with Cifelli?"

"Uh-huh."

"Just friendly?"

"Yes, of course. Why?"

"He wasn't happy when I took you away from him."

"I asked you not to refer to our past."

"Yeah, sure. What was I thinking?"

Nick hadn't meant to bring up anything personal, but she was distracting him big-time, sitting there with that feminine pink skirt flowing all around her and her hair pulled off her face with a band. Being with her was turning into his own private purgatory. Daily penance of a sort.

He sat back down with "Nato's Pics." He'd skimmed each journal to get a sense of his four and now he was ready to comment.

Nato had drawn all his entries so far. This one consisted of the kids in the support group. They were floating in clouds, and Nato had caught their expressions well: fear from Anne, desolation from Kara, revenge from J.J., emptiness from Shamika. Tommy zoning out. Carla and Hector holding hands, looking at each other. Nato sketched himself below them all, with muscles bulging, fists raised, while an attacker—amorphous and ill-defined—came toward him. Below it he'd written, "Get the bastards."

Well, there was the anger coming out. Nick wrote some words of comfort. Praise of Nato's talent. Listed some ways to channel his rage toward a perpetrator who had been caught, but was awaiting trial.

Then he picked up Tommy's book.

The Journal Without a Name
    Dear Perp,
      You did this to me. Put me in here. I hate you. I was walking down the frigging street,

minding my own business. Coming home after
basketball practice. How were you after it happened? Did you get him, after you got me? I laid
with my face in a puddle. My legs burning.
Waiting forever till somebody came. Waited for
help. Nobody can help. They never caught you.
How come I'm here and you run free?

NICK CRINGED at the despair in the entry. He wrote, "I
can never know how you feel, buddy. But I've been
helpless. When I was your age. We need to talk about
what to do with those feelings." He suggested some
ways to deal with what was inside of Tommy, some
of which related to the fact that the guy hadn't been
caught. At least he'd written about it. In the one private
counseling session he'd had with Tommy, the boy
wouldn't open up, simply moved the wheelchair back
and forth and read the posters on the wall. Much as
he hated the idea, Nick had decided to talk to Cifelli
to see if he'd meet with Tommy about his medical condition.

Hector's and Carla's journals were last. Carla's was
written in a stream of consciousness style of writing.

carved by carla
     hector tried to stop him, jumped on
Daddy's back, big man shrugged him off, he hit
his head on the coffee table, i tried to help
hector as Daddy beat and beat and beat and
there was blood and screaming and oh, my
God she's dead...

"HECTOR'S HITS" was a series of violent images.

> Cracking bone
> Screams
> Moans
> Brain matter smells like puke on my face
> Connect with coffee table
> See stars
> Don't Carla
> You bastard...I'll show you
> I'm sorry.
> Blackness.
> Still.

AFTER RESPONDING to both kids about how horrible the situation must have been and how impossible it had to be to forget the images, Nick switched journals with Madelyn. Two hours after they began, he removed his glasses and rubbed his eyes. He felt as if he'd been hit by a train. Glancing over, he saw Madelyn's face was pale and her shoulders slumped.

"Be careful what you wish for," Nick murmured. "I wanted them to open up, but reading these was tough."

"I know." She stood and stretched.

His eyes focused on the curve of her back. Before, when they'd been working on difficult things, they'd found a way to ease the physical tension. He felt his body respond just thinking of being in bed with her.

She caught his expression. If she remembered,

too, it didn't show on her face. "I've got to go. We've done everything we need to do together, right?"

"Yeah, Madelyn. We're done."

CHAPTER FIVE

OPEN HEART YOGA Center offered a 6:00 a.m. class to students of all levels. The daily routine consisted of breathing and restorative poses, which a novice could do and a longtime practitioner could benefit from. Madelyn often went to this session when she was troubled.

And today she was troubled. Yesterday's sharing of journals in the group session had been hell. The kids' entries were heart wrenching, and she couldn't stop thinking about the kids, especially how they'd read their words aloud with halting voices and in morose tones. Her own entry had been in general terms, pretty much the facts of her victimization and not even all of those. Besides the counselors she'd seen, only two people knew the whole story about her assault: Nick and Beth.

Nick's journal had been thorough. Matter-of-fact. He'd written about his father's embezzlement and how his teen years had been excruciating. The kids had listened attentively. Again, Madelyn felt sorry for the boy Nick had been, and had to fight against feeling anything for the man he'd become.

"Dr. Walsh, is that you?"

In cross-legged position, Madelyn opened her eyes to see two women standing before her. It took her a minute to recognize Tessa Logan, Nick's sister-in-law. It took her no time at all to place the older woman with Dan's wife. This had to be Nick's mother. Oh, God, he had her eyes, the same shaped face.

"Tessa, hello."

"Mom, this is Dr. Madelyn Walsh. She works with Nick. Dr. Walsh, my mother-in-law, Claire Logan."

"Nice to meet you, Mrs. Logan."

"Claire. You, too, Dr. Walsh."

"Madelyn. To both of you."

Tessa gestured around the loft, where sunlight was peeking through the open windows. "Thanks for the brochure on this place. Claire and I have both been to a class, and it's terrific."

"I'm glad you found the studio, then."

The women spread out their mats, adjusted their props and sat down on bolsters. Thankfully, the instructor rang her small bell, indicating it was now quiet time before the session began. Again, Madelyn closed her eyes and took several calming breaths. Nick's mother…here at yoga.

Unbidden, images came to her. She and Nick had been in bed once, after making love. Their intimacy was intense, probably because she'd told him about her assault and he'd made every lovemaking session tender and stirring at the same time. She was giving him a back rub; both their defenses had been lowered….

She used to do this when we were little.

Who?

Claire. Before our lives caved in on us.

You never talk about her.

Not much to say. She kicked me out when I was sixteen.

Sixteen? Oh, Nick. At least I had my mother around, though I had to take care of her.

I understand the kids from the Center, the abandonment, the lack of self-esteem engendered by that kind of loss. I felt like shit most of my life.

She'd leaned over and kissed his neck. *You're good, Nick. Don't forget that.*

Flipping over, he erased the moment. *Yeah, how good?* He kissed her.

Nick...

Shh...no more.

Madelyn opened her eyes. The woman who'd hurt Nick so badly was sitting next to her. She was the woman who had done seemingly irreparable damage to his life.

And, by default, to Madelyn's.

After class, Madelyn dawdled as she put her props away to be certain the Logans were gone before she left the loft. The last thing she needed was to socialize with them. It was only seven-thirty, so after a quick scan of the place, where she saw neither of them, Madelyn ducked into the juice bar for coffee and was heading for a table when she came upon Claire seated in the corner. Alone. Damn it, she'd missed her.

Just be polite. Stopping briefly at Claire's table, Madelyn said hello, and asked, "Did you enjoy class?"

"Yes." Claire's face was youthful with few wrinkles and hardly any sagging skin elsewhere. Nick must have inherited her genes. "I was wondering if you might sit with me, Madelyn."

Not a good idea. "Um…"

"For a moment?" A vulnerability in Claire Logan's tone made Madelyn agree.

"All right." Gingerly, like she was on a precipice, Madelyn sat.

"So, tell me about Nick at work."

She doesn't know I know. Which, of course, meant she didn't know about Madelyn and Nick's ill-fated relationship. His brother and sister were loyal and circumspect, two things critically important to Nick.

Stay on safe ground. She sipped the hot brew, wondering about how much to tell Claire. "He's absolutely wonderful with teens. They relate to him so well. It's remarkable to watch. We're lucky to have him."

"Teens are hard to handle."

Yeah, like you tried. "It's important to hang in there with them."

Claire watched her. "I know. I'm afraid I wasn't very adept at it. With Nick at least."

Madelyn made a pretense of stirring her coffee with a plastic spoon.

"I wonder where Nick got his skills."

"Experiencing difficulties yourself helps you to become a good counselor."

"And Nick's had his share. Partly because…" She didn't finish the thought, but asked instead, "What kinds of things does he do with the kids?"

Since this was neutral ground, Madelyn told Claire about the snacks, the journals, the informality that made him so accessible. She confessed how she herself envied his amiability.

His mother smiled, making Madelyn continue. Finally, she decided she'd said more than enough. "I'm sorry, I have to leave or I'll be late for work."

Claire touched her arm. "Thank you, Madelyn. For giving me a little glimpse of my son's life. As I think you know, he doesn't…let me in much."

"You're welcome." She stood. "Goodbye, Claire."

Madelyn made it to her car before a thought struck her. Nick valued privacy and hated to be the topic of discussion. He'd mentioned that to her once when someone had been gossiping about him behind his back at the Center. What would he do if he knew she'd talked to his mother about him?

It probably wouldn't be pretty. Then again, most of their encounters weren't. And if her contact with his mother kept them apart, then that was a good thing.

"Yo, DUDE. Look at this."

Nick smiled over at Nato. "Be right there." To Anne, who had a desk-sized April calendar spread before her, he said, "Here's the schedule for the National Crime Victims' Rights Week. After you record what's going on each day, can you make a sign-up sheet for the activities?"

Anne nodded. The girl didn't say much, but she was a great organizer.

He crossed to Nato who was sitting on the futon with a sketch pad on his lap. The boy's dark hair obscured his face, but Nick could see the hint of a smile. He looked up.

"Whatdaya think of these?"

Though Nato tried to be cool, there was excitement in his eyes that hadn't been there before Nick suggested to the kids that they help out with the planning for the victims' rights week at the end of the month.

Nick took the drawings and studied each one. "They're totally awesome."

Even that was an understatement. His sketch consisted of beautifully scripted lettering about teen victim statistics and a larger version of the pictures he'd done in his journal, with a lot more detail added. J.J.'s cast was accented. Kara's grimace deeper. Shamika had her hands on the computer, out of which a snake was crawling.

"I got everybody's permission to use their stuff."

"Great idea."

"Think it's too heavy?"

"Nope. You capture the essence of victimization in a drawing better than words can. You have talent, Nato."

"Whatever." Despite Nato's blasé tone, Nick detected pride in the kid's voice.

A movement at the door caught his attention, and he turned to find Maddie standing in the entry. "Hi, Madelyn."

She tugged on a silver necklace, which hung around the collar of her red cotton blouse.

He noticed the black jeans she wore fit her... well.

"Hi." She glanced at the clock. "Did I have the time wrong? I thought we said seven on Thursdays."

"We did. In my individual meetings with the kids, I asked them to come in early today."

She scanned the room. And frowned.

"Everybody was available but J.J. and Kara. They couldn't get here till seven."

Now she scowled.

"Problem?" he asked.

"Later." She donned her fake smile, which he was beginning to hate with a passion. "So what are we doing?"

At the computer, Shamika spoke voluntarily for the first time since she'd been coming to the group. "Nick asked us to help with the Crime Victims' Rights Week."

"Oh, great. Which part?"

"We want to have a teen table at the festival after the march."

"Well, that's good. We can rig something up next to the one the Center already has scheduled."

Damn. Nick recognized his error. He should have checked with her first. Of course all the Center's plans were already in place for the national event, which was only a few weeks away.

Before he could think of a comment that might placate Maddie, Kara and J.J. arrived.

Maddie turned. "Hi, Kara, J.J."

"We late?" Kara asked. Nick noticed the skin under her eyes was dark. In his private session with her, she said she hadn't been sleeping. That fact was about all she'd offered.

"No worries." His tone was easy. "Remember that I asked anybody who could to come a bit early, to help with the victims' rights week?"

Kara's look was blank.

"I said I couldn't come." J.J.'s tone was belligerent. Defiant. He held up his arm. "I had to get my cast off."

"That's terrific, J.J." Crossing to the doorway, Maddie inspected his bare arm. "Feel good?"

"Yeah, sure."

Kara said, "I'm sorry. I couldn't get here before seven." Her voice was edgy. "Can I help now?"

Maddie touched her shoulder. "Well, the session is due to start."

"Can we keep doin' this, man?" Nato asked.

"I'm in," Shamika called out.

Anne smiled. "Me, too."

Hector and Carla, who were over in the corner, looked up. Carla said, "Cool for us. We're makin' tracks on the teen brochure."

Tommy sat at another computer, his back to them. "I'm ice."

"Let me check with Madelyn." He drew her off to the side and spoke to her quietly. "I think it might be a good idea. Tuesday's journal session was intense. We could all benefit from some downtime. And maybe the kids will open up even more if we work together on something else."

Madelyn just watched him. Finally she said, "Maybe. But you should have checked this out with me."

He was getting tired of answering to her. "Do you really need to know everything I do? What's the big deal?"

"Well, for one thing, Kara and J.J. feel left out."

"I—"

Tommy wheeled over to them. "Dr. Walsh, look." He handed her a sheet of paper. "These places in Rockford provide free candy to give away and bottled water for the participants if we contact them."

Madelyn's expression softened, probably at the enthusiasm neither of them had yet heard in Tommy's voice. "I knew that. Why don't you see what you might want, make a list and I'll run it by Mrs. Baker." When he left, she glared at Nick.

"What?"

"Francy's already working on that." She waved her hand to encompass the room. "We have people up to speed on all of this."

He winced. "Okay, okay, you're right. I should have checked with you."

She sighed. The tension was obviously wearing on her, too. "I'll see that Francy includes Tommy."

"Thanks."

"So what do we do?" J.J. asked coming up behind them. "I can always split if there's nothing here for me."

"There's plenty here for you, J.J." Nick gave both kids a warm smile. "Kara, why don't you help Shamika decide which of the slogans on the Office of the Victims of Crime Web site might make interesting bookmarks."

"Bookmarks?" Kara asked. One of the few things she'd told Nick was that she loved to read.

"Yeah. To hand out at the booth."

Shamika turned. "Come 'ere, Kara. I got this idea to show books that have crime victims in them. You know, like Ophelia in *Hamlet* and that chick in *Tess of the D'Urbervilles.*"

Nick knew the chick in Hardy's book had been raped and Ophelia had been victimized by all the men in her life. A bookmark featuring those kinds of books was a very good idea.

"Hector and Carla," Nick asked, "want some help?"

Carla looked to her brother. He mumbled something to her.

"Yeah, dude, come on over."

J.J. hesitated.

Nick nodded to the spot at the table where he'd been drawing up some placards to carry in the parade. "I need some help on those signs if you'd rather work with me."

"Nah, I'll help them." He wandered over to Carla and Hector.

Alone, Nick and Maddie faced each other.

She said, "I'll go get the posters we ordered for the week. They came in this morning. They reflect the font and colors for this year. If the kids are going to do this, they might want to be in sync."

"Good idea."

"I do have some."

"Maddie, look, all I'm saying is I need some autonomy. I have to be able to read the kids and alter activities if it's best for them."

She held up her hand. "We're done with this disagreement. I'll play along today, because it appears to be working. But don't change paddles in midstream like this again, Nick."

He didn't argue further. When she walked away, he turned back to the kids. Amazing how he could be so good with them and so stupid with Maddie. Pushing back the thought, he crossed to the table to work on the signs.

"UNCLE NICK, I *found* one," ten-year-old Molly shouted from behind a tree in the backyard of Dan's new house. "And it's purple, my favorite color."

Sitting on a lounge chair on the stone patio, Nick cupped his hands and yelled, "Wait till Sara finds an egg, and then you can open yours."

From beside him, Dan chuckled. "If I tried to do that, there'd be mutiny."

"Favorite uncle's prerogative."

Tessa came out of the screened-in porch bearing hot, steaming coffee. After another restless night, a little caffeine was just what Nick needed.

Tessa set down his mug on the small wrought iron table. "It was nice of you to do this for them."

"It's nice to have the opportunity. I missed a lot of Easters with them."

A small squeeze of his arm by Tessa.

"Thanks for having me over. You've got a full day planned." That included Claire, he knew.

"Which you can stay for, Nicky." Dan's voice was neutral, but Nick knew his brother felt very strongly about Nick's estrangement from Claire.

"No thanks. Brunch is enough."

"The girls would love to have you for the afternoon and dinner," Tessa put in.

"Ah, blackmail now. Sorry, I have other plans anyway."

Dan frowned. "Which you made intentionally."

"No, I didn't. The Kramers have a holiday buffet every year. Their daughter Zoe was killed on Easter morning, Dan. The RCVC workers, along with neighbors and other friends, go to John's house Easter afternoon. I missed too many of those, too."

In typical big brother, know-it-all fashion, Dan said, "They aren't your family, Nick."

Most of the time, he could handle Dan's interfering in his life. Today, it irritated him. "Other than you and Tessa and the girls, they *are* my family." He cursed the edge in his voice. "Can we drop this?"

As if on cue, his neices raced over. Sara sidled in close and Molly perched on his knee. "We each got one," Molly told him.

"Go ahead. Open up. Let's see what the Easter Bunny brought."

Molly went first, of course. "Oh, wow. Movie tickets."

"One of the kids at the Center said there's a cool Japanese anime movie playing now."

"I love that!" Molly said. "We talked about it in school and saw some comics on them."

"Then we should go to it."

Her brow furrowed, then her eyes widened. "Whenever we wanna go, Uncle Nick?"

"Yep."

"Even at midnight?"

"If Mom and Dad say yes."

Tessa groaned and Dan mumbled something about spoiling children.

Sara cracked her egg open. "Barrettes. My favorite." She threw her arms around him. "How'd you know to get these kind, Uncle Nick?"

"The same place as I found out about the movie. The kids where I work suggested them."

And other things. He'd gotten them talking Thursday while they'd prepared posters and schedules and activities by bringing up his present dilemma.

Help me figure out what to put in the empty eggs for my nieces, he'd asked as they worked. Surprisingly, the kids rose to the occasion.

*Barrettes...nail polish...soft headbands...*from the girls.

Money...movie tickets...mall gift certificates... from the guys.

Even Maddie had joined in. *How about woven bracelets? They're all the rage now.*

When his nieces took off to find more treasures, he redirected the conversation with his brother. "How's work?" Dan had taken a job in a small office with his old law school roommate after they moved up from Orchard Place."

"I like being a defense attorney. It's very different from prosecuting." He grasped Tessa's hand, reminding Nick what had brought them to Rockford. "And I really enjoy the pro bono work."

"We have a lawyer doing pro bono stuff for us. Lily Wyatt."

"I've met her. Nice woman. She was born with a silver spoon in her mouth but it doesn't stop her from doing some really down and dirty work."

For the rest of the morning, they stayed with safe topics, while the girls found—and squealed over— the rest of the gifts in the eggs. At brunch, which consisted of some cheesy vegetable strata and flaky homemade pastries, Dan and Nick made plans to go fishing as soon as the lake warmed up, and Molly wheedled permission out of her mother and father for a midnight movie next weekend.

As Nick was leaving, Dan walked him to the car. The day had warmed up, and Nick had removed his sports coat. He wasn't planning to go home between brunch and John's open house, which started at two o'clock.

By the car, Dan jammed his hands in the pockets of his jeans. "I didn't tell you this, because I didn't want to ruin the rest of the morning, but Dad's coming to dinner today, too."

Nick felt the familiar ache in his stomach. Even though Dan had been furious with their father for his embezzlement, Nick knew that Daniel had contacted Dan while he was going through the ordeal with Tessa, and father and son had declared a truce. Nick, however, had refused even to meet with Daniel.

Dan said, "I won't apologize for trying to form some kind of relationship with him."

"I'm not asking you to. And it works for you, Dan. Just don't try and force me to bond with him."

"I won't. I told you because I don't want to do anything behind your back." He glanced away. "After what happened with Tessa, I've learned how important honesty is."

"I appreciate that. You can do me one favor, though. Don't talk about me to Daniel or Claire. It makes me feel…out of control."

"That's cruel, don't you think? Cutting them off from even knowing what you're doing?"

For a minute, Nick was tempted to tell Dan everything that had happened to him when his mother kicked him out. But the thought of uttering the words shook him. What would be the use, anyway? The sordid details would only hurt his brother and devastate Tessa. "It's what I want. Try at least?"

"I'll try. I'll tell Tessa. But not the girls just yet."

Nick arched a brow.

"Because of what happened with Frankie Hamilton—" the man who'd stalked Tessa "—we've been talking with them about forgiveness and not bearing grudges. It isn't good for them to see your resentment against Mom and Dad. Besides, they think you walk on water. I don't want to taint that."

Nick snorted at his phrasing. "Do whatever's best for the kids."

They knocked fists together. "Have a nice day," Dan said.

"Happy Easter."

Once in his car, Nick let out a heavy breath. Old emotions swamped him and he felt battered by his stirred-up feelings. Goddamn it. He hated when Daniel and Claire invaded his thoughts. He'd spent his entire adult life trying to forget about them. Walk on water? Hell, where they were concerned, he felt like he was drowning.

In a whole sea of grudges.

THE BACKYARD of the Kramers' house was completely wooded. Madelyn was staring out at the breeze rippling the trees when she saw a doe poke her head from behind a big pine.

"Oh, wow. Look at that."

John stood next to her. "And there's a fawn. Cute, huh?"

"I love the natural setting here, John."

"Us, too. We found it soothing…after Zoe."

She faced him. "Easter's still hard, isn't it?"

"Not as hard as it could be. Especially since all our friends stop by. I hope it doesn't inconvenience anyone."

"Are you kidding? We all look forward to it." She squeezed his arm. "I'd tell you if it was any different. If people felt obliged to be here."

"I'm counting on you for honesty. And thanks for doing the food this year. You and Beth. Lucy wanted to cook, but I couldn't let her. And we've never canceled before."

"I like putting my new culinary skills to work."

John's attention was caught by something over her shoulder. "Ah, there he is." Madelyn tracked his gaze and saw that Nick had come into the great room of the log cabin that John and Lucy owned. "He looks tired."

Maybe he had a hot date last night, Madelyn thought and chided herself for the little pang that shot through her. Of course he was dating. She was, too, at least in theory. "He's probably adjusting to the move and his new schedule. He's only been back a couple of weeks."

"He was visiting his family this morning."

"Really?"

"Well, Dan's family." John shook his head. "I wish…"

When he didn't continue, Madelyn nodded. In the past, they'd discussed Nick's estrangement from his parents. "Me, too."

After scanning the room, Nick headed toward them. "Hi, there." Lines formed around his mouth and eyes. But he still looked attractive in his taupe sports coat, with a navy T-shirt and pressed jeans. "Happy Easter." He handed John a bottle of wine.

"Hi, Nick," she said.

John took the bottle. "Thanks. How was your morning?"

"The kids loved the eggs. Especially your suggestion, Madelyn." He filled John in on the Easter hunt, emphasizing how the kids at the Center had helped plan the gifts.

Though it was hard for Madelyn to admit, Nick had been right about downtime with the group. They'd shared some personal information, and Madelyn was pleased that they'd allowed her and Nick that peek into their everyday lives. She wondered how Nick was feeling about his progress with them. Since there'd been no adult support group this week because it was Good Friday, she didn't have an inkling.

And shouldn't care. To get away from him, Madelyn said, "I'm going to go check the buffet. I want to put the desserts out, too. Get something to eat, Nick."

John patted her shoulder. "Maddie cooked."

A raised brow. "This I have to see."

"Try the ham. I did something special with the glaze."

In the kitchen she found Joe Cifelli and Beth refilling the meat platters and the relish tray. Beth was explaining how to make applesauce from scratch.

"It tastes fantastic. I'll have to tell Bea about it." Bea was Joe's adoptive mother, whom he adored. When he saw Madelyn, he gave her his best flirty smile. "You did a terrific job here."

"Thanks. I've come to get out desserts."

"Super." Beth picked up the platter. "I'll go check to see how Parker's faring."

"Can I help you, Mad?" Joe asked.

"Sure." She glanced around the kitchen, searching for trays, and spotted them on the open soffit above the oak cabinets. She dragged a step stool to the counter and climbed up it.

"Careful there." Joe crossed to her. "I'll watch so you don't fall."

She chuckled. "Always the rescuer." Though Joe was a full-time paramedic, he was also a city firefighter and testosterone ran heavy in his veins.

Reaching for the trays, she heard him say, "Hmm. The view's great from here."

"Cut it out, Cifelli." Madelyn laughed out loud. Before their split, he'd been fun and entertaining. "You never change, Joe. And you know what? I like that."

"Am I interrupting?"

Glancing over her shoulder, Madelyn saw Nick

in the doorway. "Of course not. We're setting out the desserts."

He held up the wine he'd brought. "I came to uncork this." He crossed to the wet bar, opened the bottle, poured himself a glass, then left without saying more.

"What's the matter with him?" Joe asked.

"Who knows?"

She handed Joe the trays and climbed down. They made small talk as they set out cookies, cannoli and brownies on smaller plates to be placed all around the great room.

"I wonder why he came back," Joe said idly.

Not wanting to share too much information, Madelyn shrugged. The tension between Nick and Joe was still there, though Joe had gone on to date several other women.

"Because of you?"

"No, if anything that would have kept him away."

"There's nothing going on between you two?"

"Nope. Not anymore." She gave him a studied look. "What about you? Anybody special in your life?"

He shrugged. "Nah. There's somebody I'd like to date, but she doesn't know I exist." He gave her a totally shocked look. "Can you believe it?"

"What's wrong with her?" Madelyn wondered who could possibly not notice the dark-eyed, sexy Italian.

"You wanna go out with me again?"

She smiled. He was great for her ego. "Can't, now. I'm your boss."

He angled his head. "Nobody would care."

"I do."

"Yeah, I guess. Anyway, you're Logan's boss, too. At least that means you're staying away from him." He moved in close and touched her cheek. "He wasn't good for you, Mad."

"It was complicated. But thanks for caring."

Back with the guests, Joe helped Madelyn distribute the dessert plates. She noticed he'd wandered over to Connor and Lily and had stopped to talk.

Madelyn had just set a plate down on a table in the corner, and when she turned around, Nick was standing behind her.

His face was full of thunderclouds. "So, are you and Cifelli an item again?"

"Excuse me?"

"He was drooling over your ass when I came into the kitchen."

"That's a bit of an exaggeration."

"You're his boss, Maddie. It's unprofessional."

"Nick, back off. First, it's none of your business, and second, nothing's going on. I know I'm his boss." She watched him. "What's with you? You're strung tight and you look awful."

He sipped his wine. "I'm restless. Out of sorts."

"Didn't you have fun at Dan's?"

"Yeah, it was great. But he got on me about staying to see Claire and Daniel."

"Maybe you should have."

"No."

"Claire genuinely wants to be part of your life, Nick."

His glass halted halfway to his mouth. "Why would you say such a thing?"

"I bumped into her at yoga."

"She's taking yoga?"

"Yes, she and Tessa joined."

"Your studio?"

"Uh-huh. I recommended it, remember. That day when you were painting the office."

His dark eyes narrowed in on her. "You said her wanting to be part of my life is genuine. How would you know that?"

Madelyn hesitated.

"Maddie?"

"I talked to her for a few minutes. She was having coffee and asked me to sit."

"You didn't talk about me, did you?"

"Not much."

"What did you tell her?"

"What you do at the Center."

"I can't believe this."

"Nick, Claire seems starved for information about you." She reached out for his arm. "Truthfully, I felt sorry for her."

He shook Maddie off. "You felt sorry for *her?* You know what she did to me. The psychologist I saw said what happened to me scars people for life. It did me, and there's no room to feel sorry for the woman responsible."

She shook her head. "I didn't reveal anything personal. Only what you do at work."

His eyes flared. "Stay out of my life, Madelyn. I let all the professional meddling go, but I won't tolerate this. I mean it. Don't ever do anything like this again."

She stepped back.

"If you do, I'm quitting the Center."

"Oh, that's mature."

"I'm serious."

"I guess you are. Fine, I'll keep my mouth shut about you. I didn't mean to share anything, anyway. It just happened."

"You of all people should have known better."

Her own temper spiked. "I guess I should have. After all, Claire's why you left me."

"Is that why you did it? Do you think that if I make amends with her, there's a chance for us?"

She was so incensed at his comment she sputtered. "Don't flatter yourself. I did it because she asked and seemed genuinely interested. But I can see I made a mistake."

His stare was glacial.

She didn't flinch. "And for the record, Nick, I'd never do anything to engineer a reconciliation between us because I'd never get back together with you. Not only did you do irreparable damage to our relationship because of your inability to trust *any* woman, but I don't respect you as a person anymore."

"Oh, and who do you respect? Cifelli? Or the college professor?"

"That's none of your business."

"Don't you like somebody messing with your personal life?"

"I got the message. I'll stay out of yours and you stay out of mine."

"Fine by me."

She sidled around him and bumped into Beth. "What's going on? I came over because you two look like you're ready to murder each other."

Maddie glared at Nick. He glared at her.

"O-*kay*," Beth said. "Seems like I need my clerical collar here."

"Talk to him," she said angrily.

"I'm done talking," he said, and stalked away.

Beth squeezed Madelyn's shoulder. "Want to tell me what happened here?"

"I just found out that John made a real mistake in thinking Nick and I could work together."

"Too late now, honey."

"Yeah," Maddie said, sighing, "For a lot of things."

CHAPTER SIX

KEEPING HER EYES downcast, Kara wandered the mall. Sunlight streamed in from the overhead glass, but something dark and cold scraped her spine. She'd come here after school and had been walking past the stores and kiosks for God knew how long. It didn't matter. Nothing did.

Tired, she dropped down on one of the benches. Ahead was a Hallmark store. Kids' birthday cards were displayed in the window. Ones with innocent little chicks and furry rabbits. Next to the card shop was a sports clothes store. Cute pink sneakers. A hockey stick. A football jersey.

Her heart started to beat fast. The shirt was orange, like… She jumped up and hurried away.

What do you do when something triggers memories of the attack? Dr. Walsh had asked yesterday.

Call someone.

Breathe deep.

Sit down and let it pass.

Kara fled to the other end of the mall. By the time she got to JC Penney's she was breathing easier.

Break the cycle.

Stopping at the food court, she bought a Coke and took a seat at one of the little tables. Staring down at the chunks of ice fizzing in the glass, she heard them before she saw them.

"Did you see that muffin ass and those honkers on the one riding the carousel?" a boy asked.

Kara didn't look up but imagined him punching the arm of another, the way guys do. They were always so physical. Even Nick was like that with the boys at the Center.

"Man, I wanna get my hands on them."

Protectively, Kara crisscrossed her arms over her breasts.

The guys stopped nearby, and she could feel their presence, hear the chairs knock against each other several tables over. A quick glance told her they'd sat—at least, some had. They were wearing school shirts that said, Fairview High Football.

Those shirts were soft, but the lettering was sticky against your face. They smelled like laundry detergent and sweat. Underneath were muscles. Big ones....

Images filled Kara's head. Awful ones. She thought she might be sick.

In the mall, a baby cried. Kara stood fast—too fast, because the chair fell back and hit the tile floor with a thud. The guys looked over, but didn't seem to see her. As if she was wasn't even there.

Again, Kara ran.

"Hey, watch it," somebody yelled when she knocked into him in front of Chock Full O' Nuts.

"Sorry."

Slower, go slower. Walk. She dug her hands inside the pockets of her jean jacket. Her fingers curled around a card that Nick had given them yesterday when they talked about calling the hotline. Crushing it in her fist, she headed toward JC Penney's.

"Can you tell me where the ladies' room is?" she asked a clerk behind the nearest counter.

"Upstairs. The escalator is behind you." The woman frowned. "Are you all right, honey?"

Without answering, Kara fled up the escalator and found the ladies' room just in time. She puked into the toilet. After, she cleaned herself up and got herself out of the stall, but she couldn't keep going. Leaning against the wall next to one of those blower things, she slid to the floor.

ON WEDNESDAY NIGHT after yoga, Madelyn returned to the RCVC; she was behind on paperwork because of the additional duties she'd taken on with the teen support group. And Nick.

Nick. Damn him. How could they keep clashing so bitterly? At one time, she wouldn't have believed they could speak to each other as they had on Sunday.

A light in Reid's office drew her down the corridor. She found him sitting in the corner in a battered stuffed chair, with a little boy on his lap.

"And then, Max said, 'Rumpus, rumpus.'"

The child giggled, and Madelyn shifted at the sound, calling attention to herself.

Reid looked up. "Madelyn, hi. I didn't expect you back after yoga class."

"I have some paperwork." She smiled. "This is Jamie, isn't it?" She'd seen the pictures of Reid's son on his desk, remembered that he was born a few weeks before Madelyn left the Center three years ago.

"Yeah." Reid shrugged, and she noticed the slump in his shoulders. "Listen, I'm sorry. My wife dropped him off here."

Madelyn cocked her head. Not usual behavior for employees.

"I know people shouldn't bring their kids to work. But she showed up with him." He brushed the baby's silky hair. "I didn't know what else to do."

"Is something wrong at home?"

"Everything. For a long time. Truthfully, I'm glad Jamie's here. I don't trust Brie with him anymore."

"I'm sorry."

"It won't affect the rest of my shift."

"I can cover the hotline until your replacement gets in. You can take your son home."

"No, he'll be fine. I'll set up a DVD on my laptop. He'll fall asleep watching it."

Madelyn crossed to the chair. "Let me hold him while you do that." The baby went easily into her arms. "Hello there, handsome." His blue eyes were almost navy. The color of Nick's. For a minute, she let herself wonder what a baby of his would look like.

If she *had* been pregnant that fateful night, the child would be about Jamie's age.

"Since you're here, would you mind watching him while I hit the john?"

"No, go ahead. And Reid, if you need to talk about anything, I'm available."

His expression was bleak. "Thanks."

Dropping down into the chair, she picked up *Where the Wild Things Are* and settled the child on her lap. He felt so solid, so sturdy. His hair smelled like baby shampoo. She was hit by a sharp bolt of longing at what she didn't—and maybe never would—have.

Jamie leaned back into her and patted the book. "Max, Max."

She cleared her throat and began to read.

Reid returned just as the phone rang. He picked up the receiver. "Rockford Crime Victims Center." He waited. "Uh-huh. Uh-huh. What does she look like? I see. I'll get someone over there."

When he hung up, his face was clouded with worry. "That was JC Penney's department store. They found a girl matching Kara Sullivan's description on the floor of the ladies' room. She was clutching our card."

"Is she hurt?" Madelyn asked, handing the baby to Reid.

"They don't think so. But she's crying uncontrollably."

"Which mall?"

"Marketplace."

"I'm going." Madelyn reached the door. "Call Nick. Tell him to meet me there."

"Good luck."

The twenty-minute drive to the mall was filled with recriminations. Should she have done more yesterday for Kara? The girl had been obviously depressed. Even Nick's coaxing hadn't been able to get her to say much.

And Madelyn had been distracted herself, upset by her run-in with Nick. Damn it, already she was letting their relationship get in the way of her work. That would have to stop.

Parking was easy, as it was seven o'clock and many shoppers had already left. She rushed inside, upstairs and found the ladies' room door ajar.

Kara sat slumped on the floor, her head down, her arms clamped around her knees.

A woman, dressed in heels and a skirt, stood beside her. "Hi."

"Hi, I'm from the RCVC."

The woman nodded.

"Kara, it's me, Madelyn Walsh."

Curled into a tight ball, Kara kept her head down and her arms tight around her legs. Madelyn asked the woman, "What happened?"

"We found her here after she asked for directions to the ladies' room. A clerk said she was upset and checked on her. She wouldn't talk to me, either."

Crossing to Kara, Madelyn knelt down in front of her. "Kara, look at me."

She shook her head.

Again, Madelyn addressed the employee. "Thanks for all you've done. Maybe you could leave us alone?"

"I'll be at the customer service desk outside if you need any help. I'll put a sign on the door so no one comes in here."

After the woman left, Madelyn sat down next to Kara. Before she could say more, the door opened and Nick stepped inside.

"Hi." He hunched down in front of them. "Kara, it's me, Nick. I'm here, too."

The girl started to cry.

He and Madelyn exchanged worried glances.

Slowly, so as not to spook her, Madelyn ran her hand down Kara's hair. "Can you tell us why you're crying?"

Nothing.

"Kara, we can help. We want to help." Nick's voice was calm and soothing. "But you need to talk to us."

"I…I saw them."

"Who?"

"The football…" Now there were sobs. Wrenching, deep-from-the-belly sobs.

Shifting closer, Madelyn slid her arm around the girl. "Who, Kara?"

"Jerseys."

"You saw football jerseys and they upset you." Nick made the observation as if it was the most normal thing in the world.

She nodded.

"Are you afraid of football players, Kara?" he asked.

The young girl's head came up. Her face was chalk white and her eyes hollow. "They're bad."

"Why are they bad?"

No response.

Sensing, *knowing* what was going on here, Madelyn cleared her throat before she spoke. "Kara, did a football player do bad things to you?"

"Don't tell." Kara spoke softly, so they had to strain to hear her.

They waited. Nothing more, only a bleak stare, as if she were far away.

Nick said, "Please talk to us."

Again, Kara put her head down. A long wait. Without looking up, she whispered, "Not you."

"Not me?" he repeated.

A shake of the head. She reached out and touched Madelyn's arm. "You. Alone."

No, please, I don't want to do this. The thought came to Maddie unbidden but very powerful.

Nick said gently, "Kara, you can tell me anything."

Kara shook her head.

Finally, Madelyn found her voice. "It's all right, Nick."

He touched her face. In that moment, the strain, the animosity between them evaporated. "Can you do this, Maddie?"

She didn't answer at first, then she nodded.

He stood, said, "I'll be outside," and left.

Desperately trying to control her own emotions, Madelyn grasped Kara's hand, then had to force the girl's grip to loosen. "Nick's gone. You can tell me."

Silence.

"You weren't attacked by girls in the parking lot, were you, Kara?"

A shake of the head.

Madelyn felt her eyes moisten. "Tell me what happened."

MADELYN'S HANDS were shaking as she hugged Kara before the girl slipped inside the backseat of her parents' car. "We'll see you tomorrow," Madelyn told her softly.

Her mother, a caring woman by all accounts, looked scared to death. "Thanks."

Kara had invoked the "don't tell parents unless it's dangerous" rule, so Nick had said she had a post-traumatic stress attack, common after an assault, but she was calmer now. In truth, though, he suspected a lot more, that was all he really knew. He'd scheduled a private session tomorrow with Kara.

The car drove off, and Madelyn wrapped her arms around her waist. The wind had picked up, playing with the hem of her skirt. She drew in a deep breath and faced Nick.

He leaned against a pole outside the store, never taking his eyes off her. "So there's more to it?"

She nodded.

"How much did she tell you?"

"Once you were gone, she admitted that girls didn't attack her. She said she didn't mean to say that about football players. That there *were* football players hanging around the parking lot that day but they didn't hurt her. They just scared her. She said nothing really happened, she was okay, there was nothing to worry about."

"How does she explain the bruises?"

"She doesn't, of course, because she's not telling the truth. She started to cry again when I asked questions she couldn't answer."

"People go in and out of denial when they begin to get to the heart of things."

"I know."

"And the truth is, or at least we suspect it is…"

"That a football player attacked her in the parking lot. She could very well have been raped." Madelyn practically whispered the last word.

"We need to talk, Maddie."

"I'm fine with this."

"You're shaken."

"No, I'm okay." Checking her watch, she said, "I have to go."

"Over my dead body."

"Excuse me."

"I'm not letting you go home alone to deal with this all by yourself."

She squared her shoulders. "I said I was fine."

He moved in close and placed his hands on her

arms. "If we're right about what we think happened to her, this will conjure horrible memories for you."

"Don't, please."

Glancing from side-to-side, he watched people leave the mall. "Come on, let's at least go to my car. Just sit a minute."

Her face was drawn. He knew her, and knew she was keeping a tight control on her emotions. He left his hand on the small of her back as they made their way to his car, and cursed the situation. Madelyn didn't need to be dealing with this.

Once inside his Eclipse, she said, "You got your car back?"

"Yesterday. A buddy of mine rushed the job."

"It's nice. When did you buy it?"

"A year ago. Maddie, talk to me."

She turned to stare out the window, but her hands gripped the folds of her green skirt. "It was a long time ago, Nick."

The *it* didn't have to be spelled out….

I want to make love, sweetheart.

I do, too. But…

He'd glanced toward at the bed, then back at her. *Something happened to you, didn't it?*

Yeah, it's why I came to work at the Center.

What, Maddie? Tell me…

And she had, in sickening detail. She'd been raped in the parking lot of the rehab center where she'd worked as a drug counselor. Though she wrote in her journal only about the beating she took, her attack had been much, much worse.

"I dealt with it all then, Nick. I got counseling and developed the coping skills I needed to go on with my life. I told you that when we were together."

"I know."

She glanced over at him. He was surprised to see a small smile on her lips. "You helped. A lot. I'd forgotten about that."

"I'm glad."

"You were so gentle. So tender. I was never afraid with you."

"I hate that you were ever afraid."

She expelled a heavy sigh. "Poor Kara. Oh, Nick, what if what we suspect is true and she was a virgin?"

"Then it's worse. But we can help her with that, too."

"I wish she could say it out loud. Could admit it directly." She smiled at him. "You'll have to be careful with her."

He didn't say anything.

"Nick?"

"I'm not sure I'm the best one to deal with her now."

Maddie's eyes widened and her breathing sped up. "You don't mean…surely you don't think I could…no, I can't counsel her."

"We don't have to decide now."

"I don't want to do that, Nick."

"She's expecting both of us tomorrow. We can see how it goes."

Reaching across the gearshift, she grasped his hand. It felt good to have her voluntarily seek contact with him for the first time in almost three years. "Nick, please, I'm better, but I don't think I can counsel her objectively. Without letting my own experience get in the way." She swallowed hard. "And I don't want to conjure up what happened to me again."

"Then you won't. I shouldn't have suggested that we meet with her together. We'll figure something else out."

Maddie took a deep breath, let it out. Repeated the process. He recognized the calming technique. "Maybe Bethany can talk to Kara, if she won't talk to you. I know for a fact that in her church ministry she's had experience with women who've been raped."

He winced at the word. "Maybe."

"I'm sorry, I'm being weak."

"You're the strongest person I know."

"Let's drop the topic for now."

He waited a bit, then squeezed her hand. She took it back. He asked, "Want to go get something to eat?"

"I don't think so. I'd like to go home and take a bath."

The words drew a doozy of an image in his mind. "With bubbles?" he teased, hoping she'd remember the pleasant physical experience of him drawing a bath for her and making love in the big tub, instead of recalling the violation she'd endured.

She stared at him. "Yeah."

He wanted her to stay with him. He wanted to take care of her as he had in the past. But he'd thrown that privilege away on a cold November night. "Sure you can drive?"

"Uh-huh. My car's straight ahead." She reached for the door handle. "Nick, thanks."

"I wish I could have done more to help."

She halted. "Being like this together reminds me that we can get along."

"Me, too."

"We have to do better at work. I'm sorry for my part in the strain of the last couple of weeks."

"I'm sorry about what I said. I overreact where Claire's concerned. I'll keep it under control."

"Well, good. I'll see you tomorrow, then." She exited the car.

He watched her until she got into her Accord, started the engine and drove away.

For a long time, he stared out the window and thought about what Madelyn said, about their run-ins all week and how hard they'd been for him to handle. But they were nothing compared to the feelings this renewed intimacy had evoked in him. Damn, he hadn't planned on that. He recognized how much more difficult working with her had just become.

"COME ON, CAMP, suck it up." Mr. Johnson, commonly known as the Nose because of the beak on his face, shouted the words as J.J. ran past him.

Ran was a stretch. They were doing a one-mile jog, a New York State qualification requirement for all high-school students every year, and J.J. was practically walking on the outdoor track of East High School. Man, he hated anything to do with sports.

Somebody sped past him. Cougar. Tough guy wrestler. All-around jerk. Gravel from the path spit up and hit J.J. on the leg and elbow, making him swear. "Watch where you're going."

Cougar turned around and ran backward. "Whatsa matter? Can't keep up?" He shook his head. "You are so gay."

"Yeah, well, you're in line for the World's Greatest Asshole."

Cougar flipped him the bird and took off.

Another person ran by. Carla Santos, from the group at the Center. She went to his school, but he didn't see much of her. She was a jock, too. Softball.

"Don't let him get to you. He's a dawg," Carla said.

"Yeah, sure. He doesn't bother me."

"Got your cast off just in time for this little event."

"Lucky me."

Carla smiled. "Pick it up, and I'll run with you."

"No, you go ahead. I'll ruin your score."

"I'm warming up." She nodded to the teacher. "Mr. Nice-and-Friendly isn't timing me yet."

"Thanks, anyway."

"Suit yourself." Carla took off at lightning speed.

J.J. hated when kids did that—tried to be nice, condescended to him—almost as much as he hated the reverse. Why the hell couldn't people leave him alone?

He finished the run with an embarrassing score of sixteen minutes. Freakin' Nose set the clipboard on the bench and jogged across the field to talk to another gym teacher.

Cougar snatched it up. "Lookee here, Camp starred again."

"Screw you." J.J. tried to circle around him.

A friend of Cougar's moved in his way. Then another.

"Nobody got lower. Geez, Camp, why don't you do us all a favor and take the bridge?"

"Leave him alone, guys." Carla spoke from behind.

"What's wrong with you, Santos? He's a weirdo."

"Just leave him alone."

"Got the hots for him?"

"What's up, Car?" Hector, her twin, with his own posse, approached them. Three guys from the street stood behind J.J.

"Cougar's being a jerk again."

With everybody preoccupied, J.J. edged away and hurried to the school. His heart was beating fast as he snuck into the locker room. His nose wrinkled at the smell of sweat and B.O. that was always in the air and sometimes made him gag. Not bothering to change—it was first period but he wasn't sticking around school today—he grabbed his clothes and was out of the gym before anybody else got back.

In the hall, he bumped into his English teacher, Mrs. Coughlin. "Hey, there, J.J., where's the fire?"

In my gut. "Nowhere, I gotta get changed."

She touched his arm, a gentle squeeze to tell him she cared. That he mattered. "You okay? You look upset." She glanced back toward the gym. "Why didn't you get dressed in the locker room?"

Everybody knew about the bullying because the two responsible for his broken arm had been suspended. "Um, it's nasty in there. Somebody barfed all over the floor."

Her expression said she wasn't fooled by the excuse. "If there's a problem, tell an adult. The school can't help if you keep things to yourself."

"Yeah, I will."

He left the teacher at a brisk pace and, when he was out of her sight, J.J. ran to his car faster than he'd done the qualifier. Inside, he could breathe again. His father used to drive this car before he died. Sometimes J.J. thought he could still smell the aftershave his dad had used. His aunt had kept the vehicle for him, and J.J. began driving it six months after he turned sixteen. To replace the fear churning his gut, he forced himself to let the anger come as he drove home. How much more of this could he take?

Thankfully, his aunt was at work. He left his car at the curb and got into the house fast. To his room. Where he was safe. Flopping down on his bed, he stared up at the stars and planets he'd put on his ceiling when he'd first moved here. He'd had them in his old room, too—his mother had helped him do it there. They'd always soothed him. Calmed him. Not today.

He tried to put what had happened out of his mind. When he couldn't, when he felt the coil inside him tighten till it hurt, he rolled to his feet and crossed to the computer. He booted it up, bypassed his e-mail and went to his search engine. The site popped up in seconds.

Into the square box he typed, *How to build a bomb.*

CHAPTER SEVEN

IN THE CONFERENCE room, John stood over the serving table and sniffed the food Madelyn had brought to the adult support group. "What is it, Maddie?"

"Shrimp cheese. We made it in one of my cooking classes." She smiled at him. "You'll like it."

"Considering Lucy's been on an American Heart Association diet, this is manna from heaven."

"Oh, dear, I don't want to interfere with your healthy food plan."

"*She's* on the diet, not me. I've been doing it with her, of course, but I can splurge a bit today."

As John helped himself to shrimp, fluffy rice and buttery green beans, Madelyn scanned the room. Nick was by the door talking with Sam Delaney. He was right on time for his first Friday support group. Wearing black dress slacks and a black-and-white checked shirt, he looked handsome. Since Wednesday night, when he'd been so understanding about her fears at the thought of counseling Kara, Madelyn had experienced bouts of terror about reconnecting with him. She simply couldn't let that happen. So when he glanced over his shoulder, caught her staring and gave her a warm, intimate smile, she looked away. She wouldn't be rude to him, but she was *not* going to encourage any suggestion of intimacy.

Everyone served themselves and Madelyn sat with John and Beth at one end of the table while Nick ate with Sam and Reid at the other. When Nick was finished, he excused himself and came down to them. "Excellent lunch, Madelyn. You really can cook."

"Glad you like it." She felt like a teenager trying not to let a guy know he affected her.

"I'm glad you're here, Nick," Beth put in, squeezing his hand.

"I'm trying to play by the rules." He smiled and Madelyn averted her gaze again. "Even though I'd rather be almost anywhere else."

He, Beth and John made small talk until everyone was done with lunch. When plates were disposed of they sat back down and passed around dessert that Francy had made.

"Thanks for coming, everyone," Madelyn said, taking a sweet from the tray. "Let's start while we're having dessert, like we usually do. Deanna, I think it's your turn to go first."

The counselor smiled. Her dark wavy hair was a mass of curls today, making her look younger than her forty-four years. "Connor and I had a court appearance with Annabelle Marks, a woman who was a client here last year. She got significant restitution from her assailant."

Most people didn't know that victims of crimes could demand money from their perpetrators, and the court could make them pay. There were also funds available from the federal government to help crime victims with counseling, medical expenses and any property damage. Some of that same federal money paid the Center's four counselors' salaries and Madelyn's, too.

"Super." Madelyn bit into a piece of baklava; the honey and nut pastry was almost decadent.

"But I have a big personal challenge this week."

"What's going on, Dee?"

"I got a teenage son who's turned into a clam." Madelyn knew Michael Gomez was a handful, but he and his mother had always managed to communicate. "Things were okay between us for a while, but now he's not talking again."

Beth, seated next to Madelyn, groaned. "Been there, done that."

Deanna smiled over at Nick. "I was going to ask if you and I could talk, Nick. I need advice from somebody objective."

"Of course. I'd be glad to help if I can. You name the time and I'll make myself available."

Madelyn nodded. "Well, good." It *was* good having him on board. Despite the threat he posed to her, he was helping here. "Anything more?"

Deanna shook her head and Abe volunteered to go

next. He was widowed and was finding that loneliness was a problem. He announced that he was increasing his private practice. "I know that's not a solution to being alone, but it's the best I can come up with for now."

Deanna and John had some suggestions for Abe.

Looking weary, Reid went next. He discussed how active the hotline—his brainchild—had been that week. Then he sighed. "I have a personal problem I've been keeping to myself, but it's affecting my work, so I want to share it today. My wife and I are separating. Long story." He ran his hand through his short, dark hair. "She's fighting for custody of Jamie, but for now, I have him. She's staying with her sister." He shook his head. "Or at least she says she is. Which I don't believe. I think there's another guy."

Murmurs of sympathy all around. And offers of support.

When John's turn came, he smiled broadly. "Well, it's no secret my professional and personal joys are coinciding. I'm getting the innovation award in Washington next weekend and am thrilled."

Everybody clapped.

"Who's going with you?" Beth asked.

"My boys and their wives. They've got some celebration activities planned. And Madelyn." He glanced down the table. "And Nick."

Beth shot Madelyn a worried look, and Madelyn tried not to show any reaction. She wasn't happy about Nick's going to Washington with them, but at least Ted would be there to distract her. Nick was busying himself with papers in front of him, his expression neutral. She wondered how he felt about the prospect of being forced into close proximity with her for a whole weekend.

A cell phone rang. People usually turned them off during this meeting, but Madelyn was glad for the interruption.

Sergeant Samantha Delaney checked the caller ID on her phone and stood. "I have to take this. It's the notification board." She stepped out of the room.

At the other end of the table, Madelyn saw Connor stiffen. Though the lawyer didn't say much, there was a tension between him and Sam that Madelyn knew was because he'd had a bad experience with the police when he'd handled his last private case. And he was aloof from everyone. About the only person Connor ever seemed to really talk to was Lily Wyatt, the RCVC's part-time lawyer. She leaned over and touched his arm. He said something in her ear.

"Lily's next." This from Joe. "How's life, Lil?"

Her beautifully streaked blond hair back in a demure bun, her makeup perfect, her suit high-end, Lily gave Joe what passed for a smile. "Professionally I'm working one of your cases, Nick." She told him about Carla and Hector's father's upcoming trial. "It's going to be tough for the kids."

"Thanks for the heads up. I'll give them some special attention."

Joe asked about how the twins were faring in their foster homes, and after the discussion ended, Madelyn faced Nick. "Would you like to go next?"

He rolled his eyes like one of his teenagers. "Why not? Professionally, the kids are bonding over the Crime Victims' Rights week. I do have some concerns about one of them." He smiled across the table. "Madelyn and I are on top of it, though."

Which wasn't quite true. Yesterday, Kara had blown off the private counseling session. Her mother had called and said Kara was sick and hadn't gone to school. She told Nick they'd notify the Center when Kara was ready to come back.

"You've got another challenge, Nick," Sam said, entering the room.

"That call?"

"Yep. It was from VINE." The acronym stood for Victim Information and Notification Everyday, an automated system that notified victims about court dates and the release, escape or transfer of offenders. "The guy who attacked one of your kids got off this morning on a technicality."

"What?"

"Which kid?" Madelyn asked.

"Nato Keyes."

"Damn!" Nick slapped his hand on the table. "He was doing well. Does he know?"

"The people over at VINE haven't talked to him yet. I asked them to call me first in case of an event like this."

Connor frowned. "Call *you?* Shouldn't I be contacted first about one of our clients? I'm the legal person on staff. A fact you seem to forget, Sergeant."

Madelyn was shocked at his aggressive tone. She'd never heard Connor raise his voice, let alone be so emotional about an issue.

"Don't get your Jockeys in a twist, Counselor. Your phone is probably ringing now. I assume you turned it off, like you were supposed to."

Nick glanced at his watch. "I should go over to the school. Nato's day ends at two-fifteen." He looked at Madelyn.

"Go ahead, you can leave now." Even though he hadn't shared anything personal, which was probably a good thing for her state of mind.

Sam picked her things up from the table. "Okay if I go with you, Nick?"

"That would be great." He smiled at the younger woman. Madelyn had a sinking feeling as they left.

Connor glared at their retreating backs.

"Beth? Your turn."

"I've got a success story. I've developed a workshop on helping church members deal with crime victims. I'm hoping to present it all over the city." Her grin was a mile wide. "Thirty people at a church out in Chili attended the first one."

"Tell us more about it."

Madelyn tried to listen to Beth's report but her mind kept wandering to the way lovely Samantha Delaney had looked at Nick.

"THIS WAS A great idea." Nick picked up the racket he'd borrowed from the fitness center at the police academy and settled it into his hand. "I need to let off some steam."

"Yeah, that's why I suggested it." Sam Delaney had changed into running shorts and a tank top. Nick had donned the workout clothes he kept in his car.

Nick rapped the racket on the floor. "Damn it. I wish we could have found Nato."

He and Sam had arrived at the boy's school to discover that Nato had skipped his afternoon classes. They'd talked to his counselor, then his friends. They'd even gone to his house, where no one was home, and had checked out a couple of hangouts his buddies had told them about. Nothing. By four, Nick and Sam gave up. She'd suggested this game to deal with their frustration levels and Nick had jumped at the chance.

"Ready?" he asked.

"You're on."

Picking up the little blue ball, he tossed it in the air and slammed it into the front wall of the court. It ricocheted back, but Sam's racquet connected with it. She slapped the ball hard, then ran to the back of the court.

She'd read his strategy right. Nick lobbed the ball to the other end. This time, she sliced it in for the first point. And laughed. "Gotcha."

"That you did."

They played like demons for an hour. Sweat

poured down Nick's face and he had to stop twice to wipe it off. Once, he ran into the wall, jamming his knee. He also got a brush burn along his arm diving for a shot. He was breathing hard and sporting bruises when they finished.

Sam was in the same shape. Bending at the waist with her hands on her knees to catch her breath, she smiled over at him. "You're good. How old are you, anyway?"

"Nearing forty. You?"

"Thirty next month."

"I've got almost a decade on you. That's why you won."

"You're not bad for an old guy."

He snorted.

"Did this help? I thought you were going to rip somebody's head off when we couldn't find Nato."

"I was. It helped."

They left the court and were headed toward the exit when a man dressed in a beat cop's uniform stepped in front of them. "Who's he?" the guy asked without greeting.

Sam's demeanor turned cold. "None of your business."

"I want to talk to you."

"Forget it, Luke. I'm done talking to you."

"Samantha, please." He grasped her arm.

Nick stepped forward. "Hands off the lady, buster."

The guy swore, Sam shook off his grip, sidled around him and she and Nick walked away.

"Problem?" he asked.

"Relationship gone sour. Man, people are right when they warn you not to dip your pen in company ink."

"Hmm. I know something about that."

"Do tell."

What the hell? He had to stay away from Maddie and Sam was fun and nice to look at. He thought briefly about Katie, the married woman he'd been seeing in Orchard Place. It had been a mistake, but they'd been close and he missed the intimacy. "Maybe sometime we'll share war stories. When we get to know each other better."

"I like the sound of that."

They reached the entrance to the academy, opposite the exit. Sam nodded to the left. "I got some stuff to do here."

"Fine."

She held out her hand and shook his. "I'll play with you anytime, Nick Logan."

"Now, how can I refuse that offer?"

Still chuckling over Sam's flirting, he got to his car and picked his cell phone off the dash. He saw he had messages and checked them.

"Nick, where *are* you?" Maddie's voice was strained. "I've been trying to reach you for an hour. I've got Kara here. She needs to talk."

Nick started the car and headed to the Center. Damn, he'd blown it with Maddie again.

FEELING BETTER than she had an hour ago, Madelyn pulled into the driveway of her house. She lived on

Park Avenue in downtown Rockford. She'd bought the home years ago before the area became *the* spot for the twentysomethings. The place was a small detached dwelling with three floors, a tiny backyard and a separate garage, all of which suited her.

She climbed out of the car and had just slammed the door when a shadow loomed over her from behind. Her heart thundered in her chest and she whirled around.

"Maddie?"

A huge sigh. She put a hand to her chest. "You scared me."

"I'm sorry. I was waiting across the street in my car and saw you drive in." He studied her face. "I wasn't thinking. I know not to sneak up on you."

Madelyn took in his shorts and a sweatshirt pushed up at the sleeves.

He must have caught her perusal. "I'm sorry I wasn't available when you called. I left my cell in the car." He plucked at his shirt. "I was playing racquetball with Sam at the police academy."

Nick and the lovely cop. Because the thought stung, her tone was clipped when she said, "You were totally out of reach."

"It was nearly four o'clock by the time we finished looking for Nato. You had that meeting with the mayor, so I didn't bother to call." He drew in a breath. "I know you want a schedule to keep to, but—"

"It isn't that. You work plenty of hours and I told you I wouldn't be keeping track of them. Besides, you're entitled to time off. But in case of emergencies, like today with Kara, it would help if you'd stay available."

Nick touched her arm. She stepped back, out of his reach. Even fleeting contact with him was dangerous.

He asked, "Was it bad? With her?"

She thought about lying. "Bad enough."

"Let's go inside and talk."

Uncomfortable with that, she shook her head. "I don't want you in my house, Nick." He'd leave his presence in the very air she'd have to breathe after he was gone.

His jaw tightened. "Then let's sit outside. It's still nice enough."

Leading him across a lawn dotted with crocuses, daffodils and a rainbow of tulips, she climbed up the steps. A two-seater swing graced the porch. She and Nick had spent time there on hot summer nights, holding hands and talking. Or necking. She short-circuited the memory. "Want something?"

"A beer if you have it."

In minutes, she was back with two Heinekens. He was seated on the swing, so she leaned against the railing.

"You can sit here, I won't bite."

"Please don't say things like that. I'm more comfortable over here." He was so sexy, all rumpled and sweaty. Even from the railing, his proximity was too much.

"Fine." His tone was angry. "Tell me about Kara."

"She came in about three-thirty. I was on the way to my meeting with the mayor."

"What happened with that?"

"I canceled. Duff is a good guy. For a politician. He realizes emergencies like this come up from time to time."

"Tell me about the session. I know you didn't want to take it alone." He shook his head. "It's my fault you were put in this position."

She didn't reply to his admission. "Kara was subdued. Said she was sick yesterday. Said she came today because she wanted to see me."

"Did she talk about the attack?"

"No, she wanted to talk about sex."

"She did?"

"Uh-huh. She asked if I thought oral sex was really having sex."

He raised his eyes to the ceiling. "Kids don't think so these days. Boggles the mind."

"I know. It flabbergasts me."

Unbidden, came images of her and Nick making love like that. A long, meaningful silence stretched between them.

"Are you thinking what I am?"

She looked away. "If I am, we shouldn't talk about it."

"Why?"

Her head came up fast. Her heart pumped. "You know very well why! First, it conjures too many images of us together. And bringing it up, analyzing it, makes it more dangerous. We have to stay distanced, Nick. I won't let you hurt me again."

"Am I that much of a threat to you?"

That made her mad. "Yes. And I am to you. We both know it."

His shoulders slumped. "All right, I do. I don't want to think about our history, either." He shook his head. "Man, it didn't take long for it to resurface."

Silence. Then Madelyn said, "Can we get back to Kara?"

"Go ahead."

"She talked about school. About not being popular unless you participated in this kind of sex... ritual, she called it."

"A ritual? Hell!"

"Yeah. She never admitted to actually doing anything. When I tried to get her to be specific, she clammed up. So I let her ramble. She stopped before the day in the parking lot. But my guess is she'd had some type of sexual contact with the guy—the football player she alluded to at the mall—before the attack."

"Which would lead her to think she didn't have the right to say no when he tried to go further."

"Uh-huh."

"The pieces of the puzzle often come randomly. This is progress for Kara, Maddie."

Madelyn nodded.

"But hard for you. I'm sorry I wasn't there to take over."

"She never would have told you this."

"You're probably right."

"I know in my heart I should be counseling her." She felt tears begin to well. "But Nick, I really don't want to do that. Today was hard for me."

"Then you won't. I'll try to make some headway with her, then consult with Beth if I can't get anywhere."

"We can go that route, but we both know what's best for Kara is for me to be her individual counselor."

"People in social work have to protect themselves, too." He gave her a wry smile. "That's why you started the Friday group."

Leaning back, she laid her head against the pillar. "Damn it."

"We'll wait and see."

She took a sip of the beer she'd forgotten she was holding. It was cool on her dry throat. She couldn't believe she was here with Nick discussing life-altering events. Who would have thought that this kind of talk would be such a turn-on? Even confronting the issue didn't abate the rush of feelings. So she tried to change the subject. "You said you couldn't find Nato?"

"Nowhere." He explained the situation.

"That's too bad. Think he'll come tomorrow morning to the group session?"

"I hope so. I went to his father's house but no one was home. Maybe I should go back over there now."

"I think you should."

He sat there, staring over at her. She saw his fist

curl around the bottle. Finally, he stood and handed it to her. "I'll go."

He'd trundled down the steps before she called out, "Nick?" He turned back. "Sam Delaney is a nice person."

"Yes, she is." He walked to his car.

Madelyn took the two bottles and went into the house, leaving the heavy door open for the spring weather to sneak in through the screen. Standing at the sink in her sunny kitchen, she cracked open the window. But she didn't smell the flower garden she'd worked on for so many hours. She didn't take pleasure in her new hammock, nestled between the trees. Instead, she saw images of young and vibrant Sam Delaney and Nick having sex, the kind that Kara had talked about.

It hurt just to think about it.

NICK MADE IT to his car, but didn't get in. He stood over it, his hands braced on the hood. If she hadn't had tears in her voice when she made the comment about Sam Delaney, he could have left more easily. If she hadn't looked like the world had ended when she told him she was more comfortable away from him, he might have been able to do the chivalrous thing.

He breathed deeply, hoping the night air would give him strength. But all he could see was her face as she talked about the rape, about handling this thing with Kara.

You always made it better, Nick.

Damn it!

The screen door slammed behind him. He crossed the hardwood floor he thought he'd never step on again, entered the kitchen he had no right to be in and found her staring out at the backyard. He hesitated, then went over and stood behind her.

She moaned as if in pain when his body came so close to hers he could feel her heat. She leaned into him. He widened his stance so her back rested against his chest.

"I'm not strong enough now, Nick. I'm too raw to resist this."

"Me, too. I really tried to leave." His arms slid around her waist. "I'm sorry."

"I don't want this. I swear to God I don't."

He buried his face in her hair. "I know. I don't want it, either." And then he added, "If things were different…but basically, I'm still the same man I was before."

Still unable to commit. Not looking for something serious. She couldn't accept him on those terms, and he wouldn't ask her to. It was why he'd left town three years ago. He'd been afraid she'd settle for half of a real relationship and end up hating him for it.

"You have to go."

"I will in a minute."

And so, for a few precious seconds, they let themselves forget what was between them and took comfort in each other's nearness. It was so easy, really. The feel of their bodies close again was familiar, enticing. In some ways, they both felt complete again, being together after a long absence. Like junkies who took fixes, knowing they shouldn't, not even knowing why they did, Madelyn and Nick let each other ease the long-standing pain their relationship had caused both of them.

NICK'S NIECES chose to see the Japanese anime movie playing at only one theater in the heart of town. He'd been in the city, near here, most of the evening, looking for Nato, with no luck. He'd finally given up, gone home, changed and headed to Dan's. Near midnight, he'd brought Molly and Sara here to fulfill the promise in their Easter eggs. Sara was sleepy but Molly was wide-eyed.

"I took a nap," she announced proudly. She was holding a huge tub of popcorn that she couldn't possibly eat all of and a bag of Twizzlers. Well, uncles could spoil, couldn't they?

"Good girl."

"Thanks for the Junior Mints," Sara said, settling down.

The movie began, and Nick tried to watch the interesting animation, which was very sophisticated. But he kept thinking about Maddie. For two hours, he played everything back in his mind. He *was* the same man who'd left Rockford—especially in the way that mattered most to her. He still couldn't trust anybody. He couldn't give his heart and risk somebody stomping on it. Despite his feelings for her, he wasn't going to hurt Maddie by asking her to settle for anything less than a full, honest relationship. And though he'd crossed a line tonight, he was ashamed of it and vowed not to do it again.

By the time the movie ended, his stomach hurt. He glanced to the side as the lights came on. Both girls were cuddled into the cushiony seats, asleep. He stood and looked down the aisle. Only a few patrons had come out this late.

He knew one of them. The big black kid with the sad smile. Nato Keyes.

Nato saw him, and Nick was afraid he'd bolt. But he didn't. He came to Nick's row and peered down at Sara and Molly. "Your nieces?"

"Yep."

"I hear you been lookin' for me."

"All day."

The boy's dark eyes were bleak. "I know about Turner, the guy who attacked me."

"I was afraid of that. How you doing with it?"

"I wanna beat the crap out of somebody." He angled his head to the screen. "It's why I came here. Midnight movies take my mind off things."

"You were the one who gave me the idea to put this one in the Easter eggs, remember?"

"Yeah. Coincidence."

"Nah. Kismet."

"What's that mean?"

"Something was meant to be. Want to talk?"

Nato nodded to the girls. "You got them."

"I have to drop them off at home, then we can chill together." At the boy's hesitation, Nick said, "Come with me. We'll get something to eat."

"I got my wheels."

"I'll bring you back here."

"You're afraid I'll bounce if I don't go with you."

"Damned right."

Nato laughed. "I guess I could. You want some help with them?"

"Yeah, you carry one, I'll get the other."

CHAPTER EIGHT

AT THE TWENTY-SIXTH annual National Crime Victims' Rights Week Award Ceremony in the nation's capital, Alberto Gonzales, the U.S. Attorney General, stood on the stage of the Ronald Reagan International Trade Center and spoke into the microphone.

"I'd like to welcome first the honorees and their families and friends. I also extend the government's greeting to representatives from crime victim centers all over the country who are here today to kick off the week ahead." He gestured behind him to the three-tiered backdrop, in the center of which was a picture of Reagan. "Once again, it's fitting to have our ceremony in this building, as President Reagan established National Crime Victims' Rights Week, and did much to call attention to the victims of crimes. Because he himself was victimized, he instituted many laws to further our causes. The awards given today were introduced by him. Recognition will go to service providers, volunteers, allied professionals, to those responsible for making public policy and for those acquiring federal service and funding."

Down the row from where she sat, Madelyn saw John Jr. holding Lucy's hand. The Kramers' two sons and their wives had flown down from Connecticut for the ceremony to celebrate their father's success and to honor their sister, Zoe. John had balked at his children's gift of a suite at the Willard Intercontinental Hotel, a place ripe with the American history he loved. Many presidents, whose biographies John routinely devoured, had stayed there. Following the ceremony, they had dinner reservations at the hotel's Crystal Room, again at the kids' expense. Of course, Madelyn and Nick would attend and had tried to chip in on the cost of the festivities. But the Kramer boys would only allow them to pay for their own hotel rooms and flights.

Madelyn was glad to be here but sitting next to Nick was torture. She could feel his presence like a smoldering fire ready to flare at the slightest provocation.

When John's name was called for the Award for Professional Innovation in Victim Services, Madelyn smiled broadly. Listening to Gonzales's comments about the uniqueness of their center, which she now headed, was rewarding to her, too. "With six full-time employees, seven part-timers and a wealth of volunteers, John's center is a model for in-house, hands-on work with clients, rather than a place for referrals. The RCVC is funded by state and federal grants and by community organizations. The Center has assisted hundreds of victims with restitution, counseling, legal aid and works closely with the Rockford police. For that innovation, and many others, it's my pleasure to give this award to Mr. John Kramer."

Dressed in a brown suit and a tie Madelyn had given him for Christmas, John approached the podium. He smiled and spoke with dignity. About Zoe. About his family. About his coworkers who'd become like a family to him. He specifically thanked Madelyn for taking the helm, which brought tears to her eyes. Beside her, Nick stirred and started to reach for her hand. At the last minute, he pulled back, and Madelyn inched away. Still, her nerves were set on edge by his gesture.

When the ceremony ended, the group waited in the lobby for John to have pictures taken with the officials and other honorees. Madelyn chatted with his children. His son, John, looked like him and Jimmy resembled Lucy.

"So, we ready for a night on the town?" John Jr. asked, draping an arm around his mother. "I'm anxious to eat in the Crystal Room."

"It's very expensive," Lucy said. "We could have gone somewhere cheaper."

"Nah. We have a lot to celebrate. Besides Jimmy's making big bucks and I'm doing okay." Both were in computers and doing more than okay.

Jimmy turned to Madelyn. "Is your date meeting us there, Madelyn?"

"Your *date?*" At John Jr.'s words, Nick's shoulders tensed under his nicely cut jacket.

She forced a smile; he was frowning. Should she

have explained beforehand about Ted? Damn it. They weren't accountable to each other. "Yes, Ted Blake, a friend of mine, is joining us for dinner."

"The college professor?"

She nodded.

"How nice."

"We're going down to this hip club across the street from the hotel for dancing after dinner." Jimmy's grin was boyish. "My mother and father still cut a mean rug."

Lucy gave her son an indulgent look. "I'll mostly watch and leave the footwork to you young people."

"Sounds like fun." Nick's tone was dry, but no one else seemed to catch his underlying sarcasm.

"Join us, Nick?" Jimmy's wife, Tammie, asked.

"Maybe."

Suddenly, inviting Ted, which Madelyn had thought a good idea to keep her and Nick apart on this trip, seemed very, very stupid.

INSTEAD OF the gnome Nick was hoping for, Ted Blake looked like Ray Liotta, one of Maddie's favorite actors, with his curly dark hair and intense blue eyes. Worse, he seemed like a nice guy. Blake had met them for dinner at the hotel and hadn't stopped touching Maddie in the three hours since. A brush of her hand. A whisper in her ear. And, of course, on the dance floor now, he held her as if she belonged to him.

"Stop glowering, dear." Lucy spoke from beside

Nick at the table for nine they'd snagged in a corner of Rizzo's. The band had launched into a slow set, so conversation was possible now. "You're wearing your feelings on your sleeve."

"I…" He started to lie, but Lucy's face was full of understanding. "It's hard watching her with him. Not that I have any right to complain."

Lucy patted his arm.

"What happened, anyway? I thought it was over between them."

"He called when he found out about John's award and asked to see her when she was in town. They have plans tomorrow night to go to the Kennedy Center."

They'd all agreed to stay from Thursday through Sunday. What had Nick been thinking?

"She didn't tell you?"

"She doesn't owe me explanations." Not anymore.

All week long he'd kept her at a distance. Come to think of it, she'd done the same. Because she'd known she was meeting Blake here? Would they make love tonight? In the room three doors down from Nick's?

The thought made his stomach pitch. So when another song started, he stood. "Let's dance, beautiful."

"I'd love to."

The melody was a bluesy one and the singer belted out soulful words. Nick tried to count his blessings. He was here with people he loved. The woman in his arms had been like a mother to him and her health was improving.

Blake's hands rested intimately on the hips of

Maddie's multicolored dress that swirled around her legs.

John had been thrilled with his award, and Nick had gotten to see him receive it.

Maddie laid her cheek on Blake's chest.

Things were going well with the kids' support group....

Damn it! Blake kissed her, brushed his lips over hers.

That was it. Nick couldn't take anymore. When the song ended and he escorted Lucy back to the table, he didn't sit down.

"I'm heading out," he said, aware that Blake and Maddie had come up behind him.

"Where are you going, buddy?" John asked.

"I like to see the Mall at night. We're only a few blocks away. Might as well take advantage of it."

He kissed Lucy's cheek, shook hands with John and bade the younger people goodbye.

To Blake he said, "Nice to meet you."

Blake only nodded.

To Maddie, he tried hard to keep the bitterness from his voice. "Have fun."

Outside in the balmy April air, Nick whipped off his jacket and loosened his tie. His pace was fast as he strode down Pennsylvania Avenue. The White House was lit up and the monuments stood proudly under the twinkling sky. He liked this city. He'd worked here for a while after he got his master's degree. Should never have left!

At the Mall, he found the spot that always sobered him, made him put things in perspective. The Vietnam Veterans' Wall. Blocks of granite, peaking up to about six feet stood as a testimony to life and death, war and peace and to the enormity of sacrifices made. Across from it, Nick sank onto a bench. There were people here, as there always were, some simply staring at the stone, others pressing paper onto the granite, taking rubbings of a name. A few were crying. Nick watched them.

And admitted some things to himself.

He wanted Maddie. He thought he'd gotten over her in the last three years. He hadn't. Working with her every day, seeing her on a regular basis, sharing professional successes and challenges showed him he was still in love with her. Funny, he'd never told her, never said those words to her. Because, he'd convinced himself, if he didn't say them, they wouldn't be true.

Hell, none of it mattered anyway. Until he changed, he couldn't have her.

Until he changed.

"Fat chance," he said aloud.

Go get counseling.

God, he didn't want to do that again. Bare his soul. Dig down to terrifying depths. Be responsive to change. The months he'd spent in therapy before had been excruciating. As soon as he'd gotten close to talking about what had happened to him in the aftermath of Claire's abandonment, he stopped going. He wanted to forget all about Claire and Daniel and what they'd done to him. Not dredge it all up and examine it. Logically, as a therapist himself, he knew he needed help. But emotionally, the man inside him wasn't ready. The grudge he held was like an old shoe, fitting well, too comfortable to change, even though it was so worn it needed to be replaced.

But he'd be stuck with it for the rest of his life, he admitted, if he didn't do something to change.

What about you? Don't you want a family? Someday, with another woman?

Maybe some day.

Then you're going to have to settle your issues with your parents.

The thought plagued him as he sat long into the night, contemplating his life in front of a testament to those who had given theirs for others.

MADELYN WAS so tired her feet ached, her shoulders hurt and her head was fuzzy. They'd stayed until the bar closed, dancing every dance. Now Ted was seated on the couch in her hotel room, holding the nightcap in his hand, the one he'd asked to be invited up for.

And he was hoping for a lot more, she knew.

She'd considered it. With Nick along, the whole trip, and especially tonight, had been unbelievably stressful. Being with Ted, letting him hold her on the dance floor, had somehow made the situation worse. The time she'd spent with Ted had made her realize how much her feelings for him paled in comparison for those she'd had…still had…for Nick.

"It's him, isn't it?"

Ted's voice brought her back to reality. "Excuse me?"

"The man who made it impossible for us to stay together is Nick Logan."

"Why do you say that?"

Ted jiggled the ice in his scotch. "Because sparks flew between you two so much at Rizzo's that I could almost see them arc."

"I was involved with him once, yes. But it's over."

"Try telling him that. I thought he was going to deck me every time I touched you."

"I'm sure you read that wrong."

He shook his head.

"Nick's out of my life, Ted. We couldn't make it work three years ago and nothing's changed."

"Then I feel sorry for you."

"Why?"

"Because, sweetheart, those sparks shot both ways." He gulped back the rest of his drink and stood. "I'm leaving before I do something stupid, like tell you I can handle your feelings for another man and press for some recreational sex."

"I'm sorry, Ted."

"Me, too."

He left her with a quick peck on the cheek. When

she closed the door behind him, she leaned her head on the cool wood for a minute, wishing things were different, wishing she cared for Ted Blake and not for Nick Logan.

THE ELEVATOR DOOR pinged open to reveal Ted Blake, standing on Nick's floor. Maddie's floor. His tie and suit coat were off and the top buttons of his shirt were open. His dark hair was askew as if he'd run his hands through it. Or someone else had.

"Blake." Nick stepped off the elevator.

"Logan." The guy stepped on, then pressed a button—obviously to keep the doors open, since they didn't close.

Nick stood there, feet spread apart, hands jammed into his pockets. He'd be damned if he'd be the one to back away.

Blake watched him. Finally, he said, "Leave her alone."

Nick just stared at him.

Without saying more, Blake drew back his hand and the doors closed.

Scowling, Nick headed to his room. What the hell had just happened? How did Blake know about Nick's relationship with Maddie? Had she told him tonight or when the two of them were dating? He passed her room and checked his watch: 1:00 a.m. He kept going to his own. Once inside, he stripped and dropped naked into bed.

He'd always been one to fall asleep fast. *You can't*

wait to block out the world, Maddie had teased. He could see her laughing, cuddled up to him. But she'd cuddled up to someone else tonight. Hadn't she?

He pushed the thought away. Ordered himself to sleep. Turned over. And over. Kept checking the red dials as they went from one to one-thirty. At two o'clock he got up, poured himself a drink and sat staring out at Pennsylvania Avenue. When that didn't make him sleepy and with some vague notion that, if he knew, he might stop acting crazy, he pulled on his jeans and stuffed his room keys in his pocket.

Cursing himself, he strode down the hall.

He knocked lightly.

No answer. Harder. Again.

Finally, the door opened. In front of him stood Maddie, dressed in a pink slip of a thing. Her blond hair was mussed and some of her makeup smudged. She looked like she'd been asleep. Of course she'd been asleep. Blake left over an hour ago.

"Nick?" she asked. "Is something wrong…Lucy?"

He shook his head. "I need to see you."

Grasping the door, she eased it toward him a few inches. "It's 2:00 a.m. Can't this wait until a decent hour?"

"No."

Again, she pushed the door forward. He stopped it with his foot. Her eyes widened. "What are you doing?"

His answer was to brush past her.

Her hand on the knob, she said, "Get out."

Pivoting, he grabbed the edge of the door and slammed it shut. Something dark and irrational was building inside him and he wouldn't—maybe couldn't—control it.

He stalked to the center of the room, and after a minute she followed. They were both barefoot, and she was several inches shorter. "What the hell is this all about?"

"What did you tell him about us?"

"Who?"

"Your old boyfriend." He took in the sexy nightgown she wore. She'd never been one for frills. "Or isn't it past tense anymore?"

"Are you kidding? Is that why you're woke me up in the middle of the night, to see if I'd slept with Ted?"

He could barely get out his next question. "Did you?"

"That's not something you get to ask, anymore, Nick."

Of course not. Nor did he have the right to lean in and grasp her arms. "Just tell me that. I can't sleep for wondering."

"Don't do this. You have to leave."

"I will. If you tell me."

Her face flushed. "What if I won't?"

"You won't like the consequences."

He saw her eyes dilate, and from beneath her gown her nipples hardened visibly. He gritted his teeth. "Goddamn it, Maddie, just tell me so I can get out of here."

"Fine. I didn't sleep with him."

"Why?"

"Nick, let it go."

He put his open palm on her chest. "Your heart's beating like a drum." He brushed his hand over her breast. "You're aroused."

She glanced down at his hand, so intimately placed. For a moment, she didn't move. Then she tried to step back. "It doesn't matter what I'm feeling right now."

He held her in place. "Oh, it matters. Sliding his hands down, he gripped her hips and yanked her to him, letting her feel his erection. "Me, too, baby."

"Don't call me that." Her words were harshly uttered. "Don't do this."

He searched for the strength to pull back. Begged a God he didn't believe in to help him get out of here, leave this woman whom he'd hurt so badly. And would again if he stayed. But it didn't work. "Too late," he said, locking her to him. "This is going to happen, Maddie."

With that, he lowered his mouth to hers.

This time, Maddie didn't struggle.

MADELYN EXPECTED out-of-control passion, but didn't get it. Nick's kiss was butterfly soft, coaxing, brushing back and forth. As gentle as he'd always been since he'd found out about the rape, he eased open her mouth with his tongue, slipped inside and explored her. He tasted like bourbon. She moaned, moved closer. Anchored her hands at his neck. His fingers pressed into her back. Slid lower. Cupped her bottom. The next moan escaped *him,* as she fitted herself to his groin. As she sank into him, hip-to-hip, torso-to-torso.

His mouth left hers, kissed his way to her ear, her jaw. Burying his lips in her neck, he nibbled her; she started, then sighed as he gently soothed the skin with his tongue.

Now that she'd let this happen, she reveled in it. Took a few love bites of her own from his shoulder.

After long luxurious moments, he drew back. His face was soft, his eyes wide and clear. "I—"

She placed trembling fingers on his mouth. "Shh, no talking."

"All right then." He slid a hand around her back and one under her knees. In his arms now, she cuddled into his chest. The dark hair sprinkled all over it tickled her nose as she inhaled him—his scent was a combination of sweat and his signature cologne. She put a hand on his pecs, felt the hard plane of muscle, felt his heartbeat. He took a few steps and eased her down his body onto her feet.

She'd said she didn't want words, but his eyes and his touch spoke for him.

As he lifted her nightgown over her head… *You are so lovely.*

As he pressed her to the bed and stretched her out… *Ah, so beautiful.*

As he knelt on the mattress, kissed her mouth, her breasts, her stomach. Lower. Each caress whispered, *I've missed you.*

Since she'd missed him, too, she listened with her heart and basked in the pleasure of the touch of the only man she'd ever loved.

HE REMEMBERED to turn her on her side so they were facing each other instead of covering her body with his. She felt less threatened that way. He grazed her breasts with his knuckles, massaged her there, then worked his way down. Her hips bucked into his palm when he touched her. Leaning forward, he brushed his lips over her shoulder, tasting the lotion she wore. Moonlit Path. He'd never forgotten it.

Her eyes were dilated with arousal. Her body was practically singing. As gently as he could, he eased into her. An overwhelming sense of peace flooded him. He swallowed hard, but the emotion kept coming. She smiled, touched his cheek, as though she knew. He could feel himself throb inside her, feel her tighten around him.

He began to move. Her eyes closed, as if she were savoring him. He continued an easy glide, in and out. She grew tenser. Every muscle in his body tightened, stretched against his skin. He wanted to draw this out longer, savor her, steep himself in her, but his body wasn't cooperating. His hips thrust, once, twice, fast, faster…

Just after she burst into her pleasure, and before his consumed him, he whispered, "I love you, Maddie."

SHE WAS DREAMING about Nick. He was in bed with her, loving her. His scent was in the sheets, and she smiled into the pillow.

Intrusive noise. Ringing. She moaned, "Go away."

It kept up. Finally she opened her eyes to sunlight. To red dials that said nine o'clock. Nine o'clock? Then she realized the phone was ringing. On her side, facing it, she reached out and picked up the receiver. "Hello?"

"Maddie, it's John. Did I wake you?"

"It's okay, I can't believe I slept this long."

"I'm sorry. I was wondering if you'd talked to Nick this morning, but I guess not."

Nick! Oh, God, it hadn't been a dream. He's right here—on the other side of the bed. And they hadn't talked. Raising herself up on one arm, she looked over her shoulder.

The bed was empty.

"Maddie?"

"Sorry, John. No, I haven't talked to him today. Did you call his room?"

"I tried. The desk told me he checked out at 6:00 a.m."

"Checked out?"

"Yes."

"Our return flights are for Sunday."

"Hmm. Maybe he changed his. For the life of me, I can't figure out why he'd take off like this. Without telling anyone. I hope nothing's wrong."

Madelyn sank back into her pillow and pulled the sheet up over her naked body. Two things dawned on her.

Last night Nick had told her he loved her—for the first time, ever.

And then he'd left her. Again.

CHAPTER NINE

NICK PULLED HIS car to the side of the road in Pitts-ford, a small suburb of Rockford, and sat staring at the white clapboard house with black shutters. It was Sunday morning and he wondered if she was home. Did she go to church? Weekend brunch with friends? She could be with Dan, Tessa and the kids. There was a car in the driveway, but he didn't know if it was hers. He'd made it a point not to know the details of Claire Logan's life.

He didn't want to be here. He didn't want to see her. But he knew in his heart—after making love with Maddie Friday night—that if he was to have any chance of a relationship with the woman he loved, he had to settle things with Claire. Nick had left Maddie again, but surely if he could make some progress this morning, she'd understand why he'd taken off with-out a word. She'd be happy. Celebrate. And she'd help him navigate this slippery emotional slope.

Getting out of the car, he breathed deeply then strode up to the small porch with a white spindled railing around it. A wreath of silk spring flowers hung on the door. His mind screamed for him to leave—all the old anger was returning. He forced himself to think of Maddie, warm and cuddly yesterday morning in bed. He'd kissed her goodbye without awakening her, and whispered, "I'll try."

And he would.

He rang the bell.

He shifted from one foot to the other.

No answer.

He rang the bell again.

On the third time, he breathed easier. There was nothing he could do if she wasn't home. As he turned to leave, the door opened.

"Nicolas?" She put her hand on her heart. "Oh, my."

"Claire." He swallowed hard, nervous and scared, wanting her approval, her unconditional love, things he'd promised himself he'd *never* yearn for again. He hadn't realized that nobody escaped that particular need.

"I was wondering if we could talk."

Her eyes widened. "Now?"

Odd. "Yes. I didn't call because—" *I wasn't sure I could do this.* "—I just didn't." He glanced at his watch. 9:00 a.m. "Is it too early?" Or too late, maybe?

Claire's hand fisted in the lapel of her Japanese print kimono. "No, no, it's not that, it's…"

"Claire? Was that the doorbell?"

The stairway to the second floor was in Nick's viewing range, and perched on the third step was

Daniel. In a bathrobe. A sense of betrayal hit Nick like a fist in the gut.

"Nick. Hello."

Nick jammed his hands in his pockets. "Are you...did you move in together?" he asked, without greeting.

Daniel said, "Yes," as Claire sputtered, "No, not really."

Nick laughed, but it was an ugly sound. "First rule of lying, guys, is to get your stories straight."

Moving to stand behind Claire, Daniel put a hand on her shoulder. "Come in, son. We can talk. No one's lying. It's just that your mother and I are still trying to work things out."

Nick hoped his expression revealed all the contempt he was feeling. "Don't call me *son*. You lost that right twenty years ago." He glared Claire. "How could you forgive him after what he did to us?"

"Nick, we all need to forgive."

He'd thought that, too, when he was in Washington, staring at the Wall. He'd thought then that maybe he could forge something of a relationship with this woman or at least take a baby step toward that end.

But this...

"This was a mistake." Nick turned away.

"No, Nick, wait..."

He strode down the steps and out to his car. Before he got in, he glanced toward the house and saw they were on the porch, watching him.

His throat clogged. His chest hurt. But the pain wasn't about his failure to fix his relationship with those people. That had been ordained long ago and Nick had been foolish to think he could change things now.

No. His pain was a result of knowing that his inability to connect with them doomed his future with Maddie.

ON SUNDAY NIGHT, Madelyn had arranged to meet Bethany at Manhattan Square to help set up for the candlelight prayer service which would kick off the National Crime Victims' Rights Week in Rockford. Her friend was across the brick area, talking to some police officers. One of them was Sam Delaney.

Don't react, she told herself. Sam was welcome to Nick. She could have him. When Maddie thought about his tender caresses and utter gentleness and how he might bestow all that on Sam, she almost choked. But she held back the emotion, as she'd been doing since yesterday morning when she'd awoken to find herself alone. Not once had she allowed herself to relive the experience of making love with Nick. It had meant a lot to both of them, she knew, but it hadn't been enough for him to stay and try to work things out between them. Damn her for even thinking that might happen.

Crossing the square, she said, "Hey there."

Beth pivoted. "Hi. How was Washington?"

"The ceremony was great."

"I hope you took lots of pictures." Sam wore her uniform tonight, like the other police officers who would be here. Some were already on duty for crowd control. Some would show up for support. "We want to preserve what happened in D.C. for posterity."

Not for Madelyn. This weekend had to be forgotten, all of it.

"John's daughter-in-law, Tammie, took plenty of photos." She forced a smile. "She's e-mailing them to the Center. We can look at them tomorrow, hopefully at the staff meeting.

Which was about the last thing Madelyn wanted. There were shots of her and Nick. Nick, who'd held her like a precious gem, then…vanished in the morning. What a cliché. Damn him, too.

"What's wrong?" Beth asked.

"Nothing. I'm tired. I didn't sleep much over the weekend."

"Why?"

"We went dancing." *I made love with Nick all night.* "Had late dinners. Went to some fireworks at the Mall."

"Sounds like a fun time."

"Yeah, swell. It'll take me a while to recuperate." But she would. She'd get this thing for him out of her system, like some minor virus, which would run its course. Sleeping with Nick had been a bad case of stupidity. Nothing life threatening.

She motioned to the square. "What can I do?"

"Pass out candles. I think Nick arranged for the kids to come early to help."

"Oh, great."

"Come on, I'll show you where they are."

They were in plain sight, boxes and boxes stacked by the table set up to hold them. Madelyn recognized Beth's ruse to get her alone. When they stopped at the table, Beth said, "What the hell happened? You look like a zombie."

Biting her lip, she tried to lie. But Beth was her best friend in the world. Nick used to tease that he was jealous of Maddie and Beth's closeness. "I made about the biggest mistake in my life this weekend."

"Nick." It wasn't a question.

She nodded. "I can't talk about it now. Maybe never. Suffice it to say, it didn't take him long to get me back in the sack." She wanted to bawl like a baby in Beth's arms. But she didn't. Three years ago, she'd promised herself she'd never cry over Nick Logan again. She did lean her head on Beth's shoulder for a moment for a warm hug from someone who loved her unconditionally. "I was so easy, Beth."

"Oh, honey. How about him?"

"He was easy, too." She chuckled.

"At least you haven't lost your sense of humor."

"No, just my pride." Madelyn drew back and pushed hair out of her eyes. "It was a mistake. I want to forget about it."

Beth's gaze shifted over Madelyn's shoulder. "Then brace yourself, because he's here."

Of course he was. She knew she'd see him tonight, had tried to prepare herself for the encounter. She'd lived her whole life taking care of herself, not depending on anybody, and she'd do that now. She took a moment to gain control, then turned around. Nick was coming toward them with four of the kids in tow. It was some consolation that he looked as bad as she felt.

"Hi," he said to Beth, then nodded to Madelyn.

"Hi, Nick." She smiled at the kids. "I'm so glad you guys could come."

Nato shrugged. "This is gonna be totally cool."

Kara stared at Madelyn. "Dr. Walsh, you okay?"

"Just fine." She nodded to the boxes. "Want to help unpack the candles?" She pretended to scan the area. "People are arriving already."

"Great idea." Nick's voice was gravelly. "You guys can start. I'll go scout around for J.J., Hector and Carla." Tommy hadn't wanted to brave the crowds.

The kids murmured their assent and began working on the boxes with Beth's help.

Nick moved in closer to Madelyn. "Come with me to look for them, Dr. Walsh."

Madelyn thought about objecting, but knew she'd have to face him alone sometime, so she let him steer her away. He stopped by a tree with bench under it. Sitting down, crossing her arms over her chest, she looked up at him. She wasn't about to make this easy.

For a moment he just watched her. "Are you all right?"

"Yes, of course. My pride's a bit bruised, is all."

He searched her face. "I don't believe you."

"Why?"

"Because I'm a wreck." He was. The evidence was in his bloodshot eyes, his slumping shoulders. Damn it, she felt sorry for him. Despite his disappearing act, she'd admitted this weekend she was still in love with him.

Which spurred a memory she couldn't quite quell.

"I'd like to know one thing, Nick. Then I'd prefer never to talk about what happened between us in Washington again. We can enter it in the mistake column."

"What do you want to know?"

"Why did you tell me you loved me?"

A muscle leaped in his jaw. He glanced away, then back to her. "Because I do."

Somewhere in her heart, which tightened at his confirmation, she believed that. Actually, if she was honest with herself, she'd believed he'd loved her three years ago. And it hadn't made a whit of difference in his ability to trust her and their relationship. "Well, obviously that's not enough." She stood. "I need to go help Beth."

She started away but he stepped in front of her. "Don't you want to know why I left?"

"I already know why. For the same reason you left last time."

His face, bleak before, drained of whatever color it had. "Oh, my God."

"What?"

"Maddie, we didn't use any protection. What you said reminded me."

Madelyn hadn't brought condoms to D.C. because she hadn't planned on needing them. Apparently, neither had he. She recognized their error in the morning and assumed he'd done the same and that was why he'd left. But if it wasn't…she didn't understand this.

"Look, Nick," she said with a calm she didn't feel. "I had my period a few days before we went to Washington, so I was only a few days into the first week of my cycle. I'm pretty regular. There's most likely nothing to worry about."

"You've been off on your calculations before."

That fateful night in November. A pregnancy scare wasn't the only reason he'd ended their relationship, but it had tipped the scales.

Well, she wasn't ringing *that* bell again. "I'm not going to discuss it with you, Nick. I'm not going to worry about a pregnancy that most likely isn't going to happen. Maybe you haven't changed, but I have. We're done with this conversation. And everything else personal. We'll stick to professional contact."

Before she could start away again, he said, "I want to know if you don't get your period."

Madelyn shook her head. "Leave it alone, Nick. I mean it."

And then she did walk away. This time, for good.

NICK WAS A SURVIVOR. If nothing else, he knew how to get through the day, how to steel himself against bouts of emotion that threatened to overwhelm him.

He'd faced Maddie last night, metaphorically kicked himself in the butt for not using a condom, then shoved that thought away, too. He simply wouldn't belabor what had happened; he'd deal with the repercussions if there were any.

A thought which wasn't so horrible in the light of day.

What the hell was wrong with him?

The nondenominational candlelight service Bethany had held last night had attracted several hundred people and Nick had taken pride in the Center's success. He'd get through today, too—first the staff meeting, then the luncheon at the Civic Center with David Pelzer. He was passing Madelyn's office when his cell phone rang.

Stopping outside her door, he clicked on. "Nick Logan."

"Mr. Logan?" The voice was vaguely familiar but he couldn't place it. "This is Abby Franklin." When he didn't respond immediately, she added, "J.J. Camp's high-school principal."

"Oh, yes. Ms. Franklin. What's up?" Something was. He could detect it in her tone.

"I've got J.J. and his aunt in my office. We have a problem, and I wondered if you could come over and talk with us."

"Is it urgent? I was going to a meeting."

He saw Madelyn come to the doorway. She raised her eyebrows and he shrugged.

"I'm afraid so. The boys who bullied J.J. are back in school today and there's already been an altercation."

"Is J.J. all right?"

"Physically, he is." She drew in a breath. "We might have to call the police on this."

"I'm coming over now. Hold off on the police, until I get there." Clicking off, he faced Maddie. John had come up behind her. "That was J.J.'s principal. There's a problem at school. I have to go over there."

"You can go after the meeting."

"No, it's urgent." He explained about the bullies and the police.

"You can't keep getting out of your responsibilities here because—"

John touched her arm. "Maddie. He needs to go. What's more, you should go with him. This could get complicated if the police are called in and Sam Delaney's not the one handling the case."

"What about the staff meeting?"

"I can run it. It's mostly a review of the upcoming week and who's responsible for what. Then we're going to look at the Washington pictures Tammie sent."

"I—"

Nick fished his keys out of his pocket. "Decide, because I have to go."

"All right. I'll come."

They made the entire drive to East High School in

the center of the city in silence. Nothing was left to say. Still Nick thought he might jump out of his skin because of the tension that filled the front seat like another passenger. He held the door into the school for her, and her murmured "thank you" were the first words she'd uttered since they'd left the Center.

A secretary led them to a big office. The principal was in a chair in front of her desk, talking with J.J.'s aunt, Anita Camp, a frail-looking woman who resembled her nephew. J.J. stood over by the window, staring out at the athletic fields.

Abby Franklin rose. She was tall, with dark red hair and an air of command about her. "Mr. Logan."

"Nick, please. And this is Madelyn Walsh, our other teen counselor and the head of the Rockford Crime Victims Center."

J.J. pivoted. "The whole freakin' cavalry's here."

At J.J.'s tone, his aunt paled and gripped a tissue she was holding.

The principal asked, "Do you know Mrs. Camp?"

"Yes. We met at intake." Maddie smiled at her.

Nick greeted her, too.

Madelyn crossed the room. "Are you all right, J.J.?"

"Yeah. Much ado about nothing." He laughed, fake and phony, at his Shakespearian quote.

"I'm afraid that's not true." Abby Franklin handed Nick something. "We found this in J.J.'s locker this morning."

Nick looked down at the slip of paper. On it was

a list of names. His heart rate escalated. He faced the boy. "Is this a hit list, J.J.?"

"Nope. I was thinkin' about having a party."

"That's a list of all the boys who've bullied him. And the three girls. The two underlined in red are the ones who were suspended for a month." Abby Franklin shot a worried glance at J.J. "The ones who came back today."

Madelyn asked, "How did you find it?"

"J.J. bumped into the boys this morning before first period. By all accounts, they didn't initiate the incident. J.J. went up to them and told them to be careful, he had a gun in his locker."

"I didn't say that. I said I had something *fun* in my locker."

"So we searched it. And found this."

"But no gun?" Maddie asked.

"None, thank God."

"Can she do that? Go through my things?"

"I can, J.J. It's school policy that we can search lockers if there's provocation."

Nick held up the note. "What's the school policy on this kind of thing?"

"Any student suspected of intent to commit violence has to be suspended, get a psych evaluation and prove to the administration he's not going to do harm to anybody."

"A suspension. For J.J.?" Mrs. Camp asked. "And he'll be home all day long?"

"Yes." The principal had obviously made up her

mind on that one. Nick could tell by her tone and the set of her jaw.

"What the hell happened to innocent until proven guilty?" J.J. asked, his face red, his hands fisted.

"We have to err on the side of protecting the students, J.J. After Columbine and the other school shootings, our board developed a zero-tolerance policy."

"But I didn't do anything wrong."

The woman crossed her arms over her chest. "That's a matter of opinion."

"Can the RCVC provide the psych evaluation?" Nick asked.

"We were hoping you would. You have a stellar reputation in the community and I know of several people you've helped. I'll have to meet with the superintendent and school lawyer before I can give you the official go-ahead, but I'm certain they'll agree to your involvement." She glanced at her watch. "Dr. Gray's waiting for a call from me."

"This is crap." J.J.'s look was venomous. "I didn't do anything. They did. They broke my *arm.*"

"And they were punished," the principal said.

"I don't get it. Why am I the one who's gotta leave school and get *evaluated?*"

"I know it doesn't sound fair. But having you work with the RCVC is the best the school can do now, J.J."

Nick crossed to him. "I swear we'll help you."

"Why should I trust you?"

"Because when I was your age, I got into serious

trouble. And no adult was there to help me. I *will* be there for you. I promise."

Finally, J.J. looked at the principal. His expression was still defiant, but he said, "Okay, I'll do this. How long am I out for?"

"That's negotiable." For the first time Principal Franklin seemed uncomfortable. Nick's instincts went on red alert. "I do have to tell you that in cases like these, so close to the end of the year, sometimes home tutoring is recommended."

"For them?"

"No, J.J., for you."

"I don't freakin' believe this."

Anita Camp moaned and shook her head.

Madelyn was watching her, too, then she faced J.J. "We're getting ahead of ourselves," Maddie told him. To the principal, she said, "Why weren't we notified that the two boys responsible for his broken arm were returning to school after spring break? As J.J.'s counselors, we could have helped him deal with it."

The principal's eyes widened. "I was under the impression you were. We always work closely with the Center."

"An omission like this can have a huge impact on our work." She angled her head to J.J. "As you can see today."

The principal looked to J.J.'s aunt.

Mrs. Camp sighed. "The guidance counselor called our house. I don't remember her saying I should call you." She wrung her hands. "Sometimes

I can't keep up with him. I never had kids of my own. And I'm not very well. My nerves are shot."

"I'm sorry, Mrs. Camp. We'll help J.J." Nick glared at the principal. "Since the school doesn't seem to be doing much of that."

"Nick, Madelyn," the principal said, "we're all on the same side here. J.J.'s."

Nick didn't respond to her statement. Instead, he addressed the boy. "Trust me, okay, kid?"

"Why not? I could use another vacation, anyway."

Nick sighed. He was going to have his hands full here. He glanced over at Maddie. At least it would keep his mind off his personal problems.

MADELYN DIDN'T WANT to admire Nick, didn't want to be impressed by his professional skills again. But he was gifted with kids, evidenced by the fact that he knew exactly what to do with J.J.

When they got back to the Center with the boy, they called Connor out of the staff meeting.

The lawyer was his usual somber self. His face was unreadable as he listened to the story, though his jaw did tense a bit. Shrewd gray eyes watched J.J. carefully.

"I'll have to check on precedents, but yes, they have the authority to suspend you, J.J." He looked at Nick and Madelyn. "It's the same as what happens with a case of alleged sexual misconduct by a teacher. For the safety of students, the school can remove the suspect before the investigation of the incident takes place."

"Is that fair?" J.J. asked.

Connor shrugged a shoulder. "It's not. It's simply the safest course of action for other kids."

"Let's make sure everybody's safe but me." J.J.'s sarcasm was warranted in Madelyn's opinion.

After the meeting with Connor, Nick took J.J. to his office and stayed with him all morning. They went out for a walk. Then he brought J.J. to the luncheon. The rest of the kids in their support group had been excused from classes to attend. All the schools in Rockford County were represented by groups of teenagers. The speaker, David Pelzer, was known nationally for his work with kids. He was a role model no one could equal.

The kids were mesmerized as he spoke of his mother, a psychotic monster who'd abused him, in ways so horrific Madelyn could barely stand to listen. The teenagers, however, were glued to every word.

Pelzer's presentation was laced with humor. "I want to talk about the *F*-word." The crowd rumbled with laughter. "Focus."

He spoke of concentrating on survival, on the day-to-day issues and not the past. He urged them to get beyond their victimization and live their lives free from its effects. He left them with a directive to be accountable for their own actions and not let the victimization and the abusers win.

For Madelyn, Pelzer's message hit home. It cinched the decision she'd been wrestling with for days.

She went to Nick's office around five o'clock and

found him sitting at his desk, his head thrown back, his feet propped up. He was so still, he might be asleep. Then he opened his eyes.

She said, "I'd like to talk to you."

His face was ravaged. "If it's about Pelzer forgiving his mother, I got the message, Maddie."

"It's not that. But I hope he helped you."

Nick dropped his feet to the floor with a thud. "What do you need?"

"I've decided to take over as Kara's counselor."

"*What?* Why?"

"Because of what Pelzer said today, mainly. He made me realize that I don't have to let my own victimization determine my actions."

"Counseling her will be hard. It will resurrect things for you."

"I know. I can handle it. Do you want to tell her or should I?

"You call her. She'll jump for joy and I don't think my ego can take that now."

"Your ego should remember what you did for J.J. today. How is he?"

"I'm not sure. I think he's adept at making adults see exactly what he wants them to see. It's going to be a long process. I set up a meeting for him with Sam at four. That's where he is now. The school superintendent agreed that Sam could handle the matter officially."

"You did well with J.J. Remember that."

"Thanks."

She pushed away from the wall. "That's all I wanted to say."

"I respect you, Maddie, for taking on Kara."

"My job's important to me."

"To us both."

"I guess."

"I went to see Claire."

Madelyn's jaw dropped. "When?"

"When I got back to Rockford." He cleared his throat. "After Friday night."

Her heart tightened in her chest. "Why did you do that?"

"Because I thought…never mind. It backfired, anyway. Get this. She was with my father, in flagrante delicto, so to speak. I couldn't do it."

"Do what exactly?"

His eyes were shadowed with confusion. "Try to make peace. At least, take the first step. But I couldn't when I saw them together."

"I'm sorry."

"It was because of you that I went. Because of what happened between us in Washington."

"I don't know what to say."

"There's nothing to say. I'm still the same man I was the first time around. I can't put my past behind me."

She waited a beat, then crossed into the room and over to the bookcase. After removing Pelzer's latest book, *Help Yourself,* she brought it to him and dropped it on his desk. "You don't have to be that

man, Nick. But don't do it for me, do it for yourself."
She walked to the door, then turned back to look at
him. And don't do it out of some misconceived notion that there's any future for us."

She left him alone in his office.

CHAPTER TEN

TOMMY DANZER landed a particularly strong blow on Nick's shoulder, knocking him farther back in his chair.

"Hey, kid, you learn fast." Nick smiled at the boy.

Under the curly bangs, Tommy's grin reached his eyes. "That guy, he was a good teacher."

One of the Center's clients, Brody Cohen, who was also in a wheelchair, had met with Tommy and suggested boxing as an outlet. Brody and Tommy had a few sessions, then Tommy had asked Nick to go a round with him today, Tuesday, before their support group met. Nick had done some boxing in his twenties when nothing short of a punching bag could release the frustration inside him.

"Is it hard to box sitting down, you know, when you don't have to?"

"Honestly, it is. My center of gravity's off."

Tommy glanced at the clock. "Can we keep going?"

Nick raised gloved hands. "Yeah, but take it easy on the old guy."

Twenty minutes later, Tommy's color was high and his eyes full of enthusiasm. Nick was sore as hell, but pleased with the change in the kid. "Great job, Tom."

"Thanks. For helping me with this."

"Yeah," he said, rubbing his shoulder, "I'd like to say you're welcome but…"

Tommy laughed out loud, full and from the belly, for the first time since he'd come to the Center.

Nick gave him one last playful jab. "I'm gonna go take a quick shower before the group."

"I'll stay here and look at some of Pelzer's books." Tommy shrugged as he removed his gloves. "It feels, you know, good to be all hot and sweaty again."

Smiling, Nick grabbed his gym bag from the closet and headed out of the room. In the hall, he bumped into someone who'd obviously been watching them through the small window in the door.

"So now you beat the crap out of the kids to make them better?" Dan's eyes were amused. He waved to Tommy inside.

Tommy waved back.

"Hey." Nick closed the door. "Inactivity for kids is deadly. Tommy was an athlete before he got shot."

"Is his injury permanent?"

"Uh-huh. Irreversible spinal cord injury. He'll never walk again." Nick sighed.

"It looked like he gave you a run for your money."

"Yeah." He studied his brother. "What are you doing here?"

"If the mountain won't come to Mohammed…"

"Ah. She told you."

"Yep. And for the record, I'm pissed at you for not returning my calls or e-mails."

"It's National Crime Victims' Rights Week. I've been busy."

Dan's expression said, *I'm not buying this.* "I know. Tessa brought some of her kids from the Villa to hear Pelzer's talk. I went with her."

"I didn't see you there."

"Lucky for you there were hundreds of people who prevented us from meeting up." Dan stared at his brother. "Did you listen to him?"

"Look, I gotta shower. My group's coming at four." He started to walk toward the stairs to the second floor where there was a lavatory with a shower.

Dan fell into step. "I'll go with you."

Nick sighed again. "You're not gonna let this go, are you?"

"No. I want to know why you went to see Mom."

"And if I don't want to talk about it?"

Dan glanced back to the group room. "We'll get the gloves and I'll duke it out of you."

"As if you could."

"Spare me. I'm in top shape from running. I can still take you."

They climbed the steps. When Nick didn't say anything—hoping his brother would get the message—Dan spoke again. "She was devastated that you left without telling her why you went over there."

"Couldn't face dear old Dad in a bathrobe." He looked at Dan. "Did you know?"

"I'm not sure what there's to know. After you met them at the Amerks game, I talked to both of them.

Last I knew they were seeing each other socially." He shook his head. "And quite frankly, hearing about their love life is *MITN*."

"It's more information than needed by me, too."

"So why'd you go to see her?"

They reached the bathroom and Nick stepped inside. Dan followed. Nick grunted. "What do you think you're doing?"

"We're gonna talk in here." Dan motioned to the large room that had a chair by the window. "Like we used to. I'll sit over there while you shower."

"We're a little old for this."

But Nick couldn't help chuckling, remembering how they used to hide in the bathroom when they were young and talk so nobody could hear them. Sometimes, Dan had purposely dragged him in there to have a heart-to-heart. For some reason, the parallel to their childhood years made it easier for Nick to open up.

From inside the shower, he confessed, "I thought I might be able to stop the pattern. Make a new start."

"Nick, that's great." The hope in Dan's voice came through the curtain.

"No, it's not." He let the hot water sluice over him. It felt soothing on his sore muscles. "In the end, I couldn't do it."

"I've never known you to give up."

"Yeah, well, I'm not as strong as I thought."

"Other than Tessa, you're the strongest person I know."

Nick didn't realize Dan felt that way. He twisted the faucets, grabbed a towel and dried off.

As he dressed, Dan said, "What brought this on, Nicky?"

He shook his head and turned to the mirror. "Something with Maddie."

"In Washington?"

"You're not prying the prurient details out of me."

"*Are* there prurient details?"

Nick finger combed his hair and stared into the glass. But instead of his face, he saw the look on Maddie's when they were making love for the first time in three years. Nothing had ever felt so right.

He turned to his brother. "We hooked up. I…" He shook his head. "I realized I'm still in love with her. I thought if I made some overture to Claire, tried to deal with my problems, Maddie and I might…" He shrugged, that little boy again, telling his secrets to his older brother in the bathroom. "I couldn't do it, so it doesn't matter."

"I think it matters. I think it's a big step. But you need more."

"More what?"

"Counseling. What about the guy you saw here after you left and before you came to Orchard Place?"

"Didn't work. When I started to get to the real issues, I quit."

"Is there someone at the Center you could talk to? Does anybody have a private practice?"

Abe Carpenter did. And Nick respected him. "Yeah, but I don't know, Dan, I think I'm a hopeless case."

"If you think you are…"

"I know, then I am." He glanced at his watch, embarrassed because he mouthed that sentiment to his teenagers all the time. "I gotta go. The kids'll be coming in soon."

Dan stood and blocked the door. "Say you'll think about getting some help." And again, like when they were kids, he finished, "I won't let you out until you do."

"Yeah, you and what army?" They both laughed. "All right, I'll think about it."

Dan socked him on the arm. "Nice talkin' to you, buddy."

Nick snorted. "You're a piece of work, you know that?

"You, too."

Musings by Anne
    She feels important. Like some of the clouds drifted away. She's good at something, helping others in the support group, organizing things. Being able to contribute. The speaker's story yesterday was so sad. Her problems are nothing compared to his. She's feeling better for the first time since the man crashed into their house and practically ruined the life of everyone in her family.

Kara's Journal
    Maybe I can.
    Maybe it's not hopeless.

She seems to care
Even if she can never understand.
No one can
But having an ally…
Who really listened,
Who heard,
Who said everything would work out.
I almost believed her.

Jonesing about J.J.

The dude's chunk, so maybe some adults aren't total shitheads. He told me all that stuff about his father, about how he hated the world. Freak! He even spent some time inside when he wasn't much older than me. His life sucked; he hit bottom. Ain't gonna happen to me, though. Ain't gonna let anybody get the drift on me. Decided to talk to him. Kinda like being with him. Like a father. Funny, since his own pop was such a loser.

SHAMIKA'S HOME PAGE

2DAY IS OK. HELPED. THE COMP IS A FRIEND. NO FRIEND ON IT THOUGH NEMORE. WILL GO TO THE THING 2MORONITE. SOME1 TO GO WITH FINALLY. LEAST 1 GOOD THING.

Tommy's Journal

Dear Nick,

Thanks for doing that for me—getting that guy Brody to talk to me, and then boxing with me today. Doesn't make this suck any less, but it helped. Don't feel like I'm gonna combust anymore. Sorry about those left jabs (ha ha). For the first time in months, I felt athletic. Did you know I played b-ball? I wouldn't talk about it 'cause it hurt too much. Brody was cool, too. Said I'd get used to being in the chair, but the frustration would probably never go away completely. Least he was honest…

carved by carla
    he's going to trial, the lawyer says he'll get convicted, they got a body and two eye-witnesses, we're gonna have to testify me and hec, I can do it but he can't, I'm worried about him, nick, madelyn can you help oh, btw I think it sucks about J.J.—we go to the same school, you know, kids are always calling him names, those guys came back and J.J. got kicked outta school, it's not right, why isn't life fair?

Hector's Hits

    The good…
    I did the brochure
    I like it here, makes me feel calm

    The bad…
    School sucks
    The place needs a serious overhaul.

    The ugly…
    The old man is going to trial
    Going to jail

> I gotta help put him there
> What kinda world is this?

"Nato's Pics" was a series of images: candles, flickering so vividly you could almost feel their heat…David Pelzer, drawn with such detail you thought he might step off the page…the Center with its doors wide-open…Nick and Madelyn side-by-side, smiling out from inside…

Nick's journal—for my eyes only
The kids are doing well, thanks largely to Maddie. She's got such courage, so much more than I have. I'm shamed by all of them. Pelzer was right. Can't let the victimization continue to victimize you. What to do? Dan came down hard. Like always. He should. But I choked when I saw my…say it, Nick. Utter the words, if only in this journal. He's your father and she's your mother. It's time to do something. Time to see somebody or this'll never go away. And maybe I'll be able to look these kids in the eye when I tell them they have to find a way to deal with their issues.

Looming, of course—are you pregnant, Maddie? With my child? And how do I really feel about that?

THE APRIL MORNING in Rockford was crystal clear and beautiful in honor of the March for Justice, the culmination of National Crime Victims' Rights Week. Similar events were taking place all over the country.

"This is way cool," Kara said from beside Madelyn. "Look at all the people who came out."

Not only had hundreds gathered to make the trek itself but there were spectators lining the route from the RCVC to Highland Park Crime Victims Memorial. "I know. Every year, I'm thrilled by the support."

"You like doing this?" Kara peeked out from behind her placard which read, Validate Victims' Voices. "Working at the Center?"

"I love it. I can't think of a better career."

"Can I ask you something?"

"Of course."

"Are you married?" She glanced at Madelyn's hands. "You don't wear a ring."

"No, Kara, I'm not married."

"How come? You're what, thirty-five?"

"Closer to forty. I guess I haven't found the guy for me yet."

"Do you want kids?"

She placed a hand on her stomach. "Yes." Still too early to know if she was pregnant. She wasn't really concerned, but Nick had spooked her into thinking about it.

From a row of people a few feet over, Anne called out, "Dr. Walsh, look."

Maddie tracked the direction of Anne's pointed finger. Behind them, Nick and Nato were taking up the rear with a banner that Nato had made. He'd drawn all the kids from the group on it, again with their permission to display it publicly, but no one had seen the completed project. Below was lettered, Talk to Teens about Crime. The plan was to attach it to the Center's teen table in Highland Park where the festival would be held after the march.

"Wow, *realment grande*." Carla smiled. "Really mag." She watched them. "How come the boys are all together?"

"Must be a guy thing." Maddie smiled. "It's so nice that Tommy's with them. I think it's important for people to see him and for him to be with us."

The only group member not marching was Shamika. She'd volunteered to sit at the booth until the rest of them arrived at their destination. Madelyn suspected that, because of her weight, she couldn't walk for a mile.

The marchers began to sing, "We Shall Overcome," which happened every year. Beth, who was up ahead with Sam and Joe and John, turned around and smiled at Madelyn. Some of the staff was setting up the Center's table, but several were walking.

They reached the memorial, which consisted of a huge granite headstone and a dedication that read: "To the fallen victims of crime. You will never be forgotten." A garden had been planted around it and bloomed brightly as if to counter the sad memories.

Beth walked to the raised podium, poised and smiling with the sun behind her. She talked about the memorial and how it had been erected with taxpayers' money years ago. She stated simply what people could learn from it. And she ended with a prayer.

"Spirit above and within, help us always to remember that there is evil in the world, evil that causes victimization but you are there to help us all cope. In whatever form you come to us, as a heavenly father or mother, as Buddha or Mohammed, as gods or goddesses of the earth, let us have faith in you and your ability to help us all make the world a better place."

Murmurs of "Amen" rumbled through the huge crowd.

When people disbanded to find their booths and tables, or wandered around to see the displays, Madelyn and the kids headed to the Center's designated spot.

Lily was behind the adult table, looking like a spring flower in green and yellow. Shamika had gotten the kids' table set up and her smile was animated. Both offered handouts: brochures, cards with candy attached giving the Center's contact information, buttons the kids had made on the computer whose messages reiterated the signs they'd carried. And, of course, Shamika's literary bookmarks. It took a minute to tack up Nato's poster and place the placards all around the booth, but in a short time they were ready to talk to people about the RCVC.

Two of the Center's counselors approached them. Deanna Gomez had been walking around with Abe Carpenter to look at the other displays and information on the services for crime victims available in

Rockford. Interspersed were food kiosks and some vendors selling wares.

"Hey there," Deanna said. "This looks great. She checked out the kids' table. "Wow, this is the best booth we've seen."

Hector smiled broadly. "Nato did the artwork."

"You got talent, boy," Abe said. He looked around. "Where's Nick?"

"He's getting Tommy over here."

"When do we eat?" J.J. asked. "I'm starved."

"Anytime." Maddie pointed behind them. "Why don't you drag the coolers over to that empty picnic table and get set up."

When several of the kids complied, Deanna smiled. "They're doing great, Maddie."

"Today." All mental health workers knew success was day-to-day. "How's your son?"

"Michael's doing better. My brother is bringing him to meet me here for lunch." Deanna winked at her. "Time for you two to meet, I'd say."

For months, Deanna had been trying to fix up Madelyn and her brother, Rafael. Maddie knew it was time to move on. Seeing Rafe might help her along that path. "Sounds good to me."

"What does?" Nick had come up to them after he wheeled Tommy over to the picnic table.

"I've been trying to hook Madelyn up with my brother. He'll be here today."

Nick said, "Ah, another one," and walked away.

Abe and Deanna exchanged looks. Abe asked, "What was that all about?"

Madelyn shook her head. "Who knows?"

A crowd of people approached the booth all at once. Maddie was glad for the distraction. She handed out brochures and talked to visitors. Mayor Duff stopped by and they took a promotional photo of him and John and Madelyn. Duff was particularly interested in the kids' table and gave them high praise. He also had a photo taken with them. It was fun seeing the kids acting like normal teenagers: jockeying for the best spot, putting horns with their fingers behind each other's heads, making jokes about ugly pusses breaking the camera.

Madelyn was feeling better as she turned to another group who approached her table. It was Dan, Tessa, the girls…and Nick's mother, Claire.

NICK WAS RAZZING the boys about hogging all the side dishes that went with the chicken they'd brought from a fast-food place when Tommy tapped his shoulder. "Hey, Nick, isn't that the guy who came to see you at the Center the other day when we were boxing?"

Dan was here?

Nato added, "Those are your nieces."

Wiping sticky hands on a napkin, Nick glanced over his shoulder. "Yeah, that's my brother and his wife."

"Who's the other lady?" J.J. asked.

"What other lady?"

"The older one. Talking to Madelyn."

Dan moved, clearing Nick's line of vision. Madelyn was bent over the table, her head near Claire's, pointing something out in a brochure. He froze at the sight of the two of them together.

"Who is it, Nick?" Hector asked.

"That's Claire, my...mother." Though he practically choked on the word, it came out almost normal.

He turned back to the food and noticed J.J. was watching him.

I left home when I was sixteen.

Why?

My mother gave me an ultimatum.

What happened to you?

Things I can't talk about. Even now.

You see her?

No. And that's a bad role model for you.

Why?

Long story. I'm working on it though.

Remembering the words, Nick ordered himself to stand. "I'm going to go say hi." He crossed the grass feeling as if he was headed to the gallows. His palms were sweaty and his heart was beating fast. Nobody understood what facing Claire was like for him.

"Uncle Nick," Molly shouted and ran toward him, leaping into his arms, hugging him around the neck. He held on to her until they reached the others.

"Hi, everybody."

Tessa kissed him. "Hey, stranger." She waved to

indicate their tables. "You guys did a great job. Especially with the kids' section."

"All their doing." He made himself look at her. "Hello, Claire."

"Nick. How are you?"

"Enjoying this."

Or at least he had been. No, no, he wouldn't let that happen. He'd told the teens he worked with over and over that someone could spoil something for you only if you let them.

He smiled down at his nieces. "The fire department's selling ice cream over there. Want some?"

They chimed yes in unison.

He caught a glimpse of Madelyn's face. It was sad. His gaze dropped to her stomach. What if… He turned his head and J.J. came into view. Suddenly, Nick knew…he *knew*…he should ask his mother to go with them to get ice cream. It was such a little thing. Start the process, begin to bridge the gap. Maddie would see, J.J. would see…

But he couldn't do it. He just couldn't.

So he took his nieces by the hands and left. He felt his own weakness, his shortcomings, as though they were walking beside him and the girls.

Damn it.

Later, when his family had gone, he was sitting on top of the picnic table and saw that Abe was alone behind the booth. Without analyzing what he was doing, he got up and strode over. "Hi, Abe."

"Nick." The older man studied him. "You okay? You seem on edge."

"No, I'm not okay. I was wondering if…" He jammed his hands in his pockets. *God, this was hard.* "I was wondering if you'd consider seeing me."

"Seeing you?"

"Professionally. As part of your private practice. I need some counseling." His heart beat faster in his chest and his head felt light. "ASAP."

"I'd be glad to, Nick." Abe checked his watch. "I've got some free time later this afternoon. Or do you have plans?"

Looking toward the horizon, Nick saw Maddie and Deanna standing with a guy—Deanna's brother? He was handsome. Rugged. And he was looking at Madelyn like she was tonight's dessert.

"No, no plans." He turned back to Abe. "This afternoon would be great."

CHAPTER ELEVEN

KARA PERCHED on the futon in the support-group room, leafing through the pages of the magazine in her lap. She didn't want to look at Madelyn—after three sessions she no longer called her Dr. Walsh—because she knew she'd see disappointment in the counselor's eyes.

She was disappointed in herself.

"Kara, talk to me."

She dragged her gaze away from *Teen People*. Madelyn was so pretty. Today she was wearing a pink shirt and slacks to match. Her blond hair fell in fluffy waves around her face. "You look nice today."

"Thank you." When nothing more was forthcoming, Madelyn asked, "How's school?"

"Okay." *Horrible.*

"Forgive me, I don't believe you."

Kara started. Madelyn had never said anything like that, in that tone of voice, before.

"Honey, I can't help you if you don't talk to me, if you don't tell me the truth."

At the thought of the truth, Kara's stomach felt

nauseous. It happened every time she even considered talking about what had really happened to her. Her mother had tried a thousand times to get her to talk about the incident, but she couldn't. She felt the tears began to course down her cheeks.

Madelyn slid off the chair, sat next to her and put her arm around Kara. She smelled like some lotion her mother wore. "If you get it out, if you say the words, that knot inside you will ease."

Kara buried her face in Madelyn's shirt. For a minute, she felt safe. "I—I—" she wouldn't look up, couldn't "—I don't know how to say it."

"Let's do this. I'll ask you questions. You answer. Try to use more than one syllable."

Kara nodded.

"You were assaulted, we know that much because of your bruises. Did it happen in the parking lot at school?"

"Sort of."

"You told us initially you were attacked by a group of girls. Were you?"

"N-no. I lied."

"Why did you lie, honey?"

"Because I was ashamed. And scared."

Her face was still averted so she saw Madelyn grip the tablet on her lap. "What were you ashamed of?"

"Of what happened."

"Victims are not at fault, Kara. That's the cardinal rule of this place."

"I know. But I…deserved this."

"No! Whatever happened, you didn't deserve it." She heard Madelyn sigh. "Were football players involved? Remember, you mentioned them at the mall?" When Kara hesitated, Madelyn added, "Or maybe one."

Kara tried to take in breaths, panicked when she couldn't. Her heart began to beat fast. Her head felt light. "I—I can't breathe."

"Sit up. Now lean over." Madelyn pushed Kara's head down between her knees. "You're hyperventilating. It's okay. It'll pass." Her hand made soothing circles on Kara's back and she crooned comforting words.

Finally, Kara could breathe again. She straightened up.

Madelyn said, "That was an anxiety attack. Do you get them often?"

"When I think about this. Especially when I tried to talk to my mother about it."

"Talk to *me*. What happened that you think you deserved?"

She was so tired, *so* tired of being alone in this, of hating herself for what had happened. Last night, she'd seen the pills in the bathroom medicine cabinet; taken them out, one bottle at a time; and gripped them until she was dizzy. But Kara realized one thing, at least. Dying was worse than talking.

"His name is Eric Zacko. He's the quarterback of the football team."

"And you saw him in the parking lot at school that day."

"I—I met him there intentionally. And other places."

Madelyn's hand soothed Kara's arm. "Did you get in his car?"

"Uh-huh."

"What happened, Kara?"

"You know."

"I think I do. I think I know everything. But you have to say it out loud."

Still, she waited. Finally, "He paid attention to me, you know, in school. I'm seventeen years old and no other boy ever did. Then I started meeting him. He said nobody could know, we were so different and the guys wouldn't understand. But I didn't care. I liked his kisses." She hesitated, wondering how far to go. "The other stuff, I didn't like so much."

"What was that?"

"I went down...I did the oral sex thing, like I asked you about before. Only he said it really wasn't sex and I was still a virgin."

Her mouth went dry thinking about what she'd done. She'd hated doing it. It was nasty and scary and made her feel bad. Her mother said once, if you did something and you felt bad inside, that's how you knew it was wrong. Her mother would be ashamed of Kara, too, if she knew.

"Did he force you to do perform oral sex on him, Kara?"

Tell. Tell. Tell.

"No." But she added, "He didn't force me to do *that*."

Because she was still looking down, Kara saw Madelyn's knuckles were white, she was fisting her hand so tight. "What *did* he force you to do?"

"Promise you won't tell anybody?"

"I have to tell Nick. Since you're seventeen, we aren't required to tell anybody else unless you give us your permission."

"Okay." She took in a deep breath. "He wanted to have real sex, he said. That day I met him in the parking lot. We drove to Rocky Cove." A favorite make-out spot on the lake. Nobody had ever taken her there before.

"Go on."

"At first I said yes. I'd...do it. But when he started to take off my clothes, I got scared. So I..."

Wait...don't.

Come on, Kara. We already did stuff.

You said that wasn't sex.

Who gives a shit what it was? Are we gonna get busy or not?

I'm a virgin, Eric.

Hell, nobody's ever gonna care about that.

She didn't answer. He pulled up her skirt. The air was cold and he shoved her against the seat.

No, don't. I don't want to.

Too late now, babe.

She wrenched back and banged her shoulder

against the door. He gripped her arms. She tried to get away. A blow landed hard on her cheek. Another.

Her head swam. She stopped struggling.

The pain...oh, God, it hurts so much.

"It hurts. Stop. Please stop."

Suddenly, she realized where she was—not in Eric's car, but at the crime victims center. Safe.

Madelyn was kneeling in front of her, holding her hands. "Did he stop?"

Kara shook her head.

"Say it out loud."

"He didn't stop. He hit me hard." She gulped for breath. "He forced me to have sex. After I said no."

"He raped you, Kara." Madelyn's voice was raw. Her face was chalk white.

"Yeah, he raped me."

Madelyn bit her lip.

"You knew, didn't you?" Kara's voice was soft.

"Yes. And now *you* know." At the girl's questioning look, Madelyn added, "You know he raped you. You know, even at the last minute, you had a right to say no."

"Did I?"

"Absolutely. In your heart, I think you've always known that."

Kara sighed. "Maybe. I'm so tired." She closed her eyes, leaned her head against the cushion. "Do we have to talk about this more? I feel sick inside."

"Not now. But we'll need to talk eventually."

"About what?"

A slight hesitation. "Mostly about what you're feeling."

"I feel shitty."

Madelyn stood. "We won't talk about it anymore today, but I don't want you to go home yet."

"Why?"

"Because you just did something very brave, and very right, but very scary. Admitting this is a huge deal and I'm proud of you. However, we never know how we're going to react after a session like this."

Kara glanced at the clock. "My mother's picking me up in fifteen minutes."

"Let's call her. Tell her you're going to help me out with some filing. If she can't come get you later, I'll drive you home."

"I'd like that."

"Me, too." Madelyn smiled, but there were shadows in her eyes that Kara hadn't noticed before.

Kara realized it hurt Madelyn to hear she'd been raped. For some reason, that comforted her. If Madelyn could be hurt by just hearing about what had happened to her at Rocky Cove, it *was* a big deal and she hadn't made too much of it.

They opened the group session room door just as J.J. and Nick reached it.

Nick smiled at them. "Hey, there. You done in here? If not, we can use my office."

"We're done," Madelyn told him. Her voice sounded raspy.

"Everything all right?"

"Great. Kara's going to help me with filing."

Nick didn't move, just watched Madelyn for a minute. "I'll check in with you after J.J. and I are done."

As Kara followed Madelyn out, she wondered why Nick was staring at them so funny.

"WHAT'S WITH them?" J.J. asked.

"Excuse me?"

"Kara and Madelyn. They were really bummed."

"Sometimes, counseling sessions drain you." Nick glanced to the door. "Especially when you have breakthroughs."

"Guess we haven't had one of those yet."

"Why do you say that?"

"I don't feel like they look."

"Maybe that's because you haven't been telling me anything important, buddy."

J.J. shrugged one shoulder and dropped down on a beanbag chair. "When am I going back to school?"

"You're on a week's suspension. We have a meeting with your principal on Tuesday. She's waiting for a recommendation from me."

"What are you gonna tell her?"

"There's not much to say, is there?"

The dude was right. J.J. had been bullshitting all week. He wanted to confide in Nick, but could you really trust anybody to watch your back?

"You can trust me, J.J."

"Because you got your own crap to deal with?"

Give the guy credit, he covered good. But J.J.

recognized the emotions in Nick's eyes. Confusion, fear, anger were all there every time he talked about his childhood.

Nick's reaction loosened something inside J.J. "Here's the deal. You tell me one thing, really important, like you did before, and I'll tell you the same kind of thing." J.J said.

"Okay. I'm getting some counseling myself. To deal with the issues in my past."

"How come?"

"Because I'm sick of living like I have been. Besides, I feel like a hypocrite, asking you guys to get everything out in the open and talk about it, then keeping my stuff in."

That was cool.

"Your turn."

He held Nick's gaze. "It wasn't a hit list."

"No?"

"It was a scare list. I wanted somebody to find it. To, you know, scare them so they'd leave me alone."

"Is this the truth, J.J.?"

It was. "I swear to God."

After he'd researched bomb building on that Web site, he'd bought all the materials and figured out how to put one together. He'd assembled it, complete with figuring out a crude timer, then taken the whole thing apart and left all the stuff stored in the basement where his aunt never went. Because he knew he couldn't blow anything or anybody up. He couldn't hurt people like that. But he had to do *something*. Nick and Madelyn had talked about taking control, so this was his way to do it. He told Nick that.

Nick shook his head, in that way adults have when kids freak them out. "We didn't mean for you to do *this*, J.J."

"It worked, didn't it? People took me seriously."

"Very seriously. Enough, maybe, to keep you out of school the rest of the year."

His fists curled. That couldn't happen. "Franklin said the suspension was temporary."

"She said there was the possibility of home tutoring."

"I don't want that." He started to sweat. "Cripes, my aunt would freak having me around for the rest of the school year. She's been cuckoo all week since I've been home."

"Then you'll have to talk to Ms. Franklin and tell her what happened. What you were trying to do."

J.J. leaned back in his chair. "Think she'll believe me?"

"I don't know."

"Do you?"

"About this, yeah. I am worried that if something else happens, you'll go off half-cocked."

J.J.'s throat felt tight. He was worried about that, too. "C-can I keep seeing you, like this? Then if things get weird, I'll be able to talk to you."

"That's music to my ears, buddy. So on Tuesday we'll try to convince Ms. Franklin that you're okay."

CALL BETH. You don't have to deal with this alone.

Madelyn sat in her office, blinds closed, lights off, only a tiny beam filtering in from the parking lot. She was trying to figure out how to handle all the emotions bubbling inside her. The adrenaline rush had peaked and Madelyn had crashed an hour after Kara left. Then, a headache had begun, starting at her neck and shooting pain through her skull. Closing her eyes, she'd put her head down on the desk. But that hadn't help. She could see him, like Kara could see Eric Zacko....

He'd jumped out of the bushes, behind her.

Pushed her to the ground.

He'd smelled like booze and body odor. She'd gagged, and he'd slapped a hand over her mouth.

Big. He was really big. And heavy.

She struggled, so he knocked her hard on the side of the head more than once. The crisis counselors said that was a blessing because she was woozy during the whole thing.

Still, she felt his clammy hands, the bolt of lightning-sharp pain at the awful violation. The next thing she remembered clearly was the police and ambulance arriving.

And today, somewhere in her unconscious, she'd relived it all.

"Madelyn?"

Oh, God, she'd thought Nick had gone. After J.J. left, he'd checked in with her while she'd been with Kara. He'd gone to a meeting with Hector and Carla at the district attorney's office, but he must have come back to the Center.

"Are you all right?"

Slowly, as if her head weighed a thousand pounds, she straightened. "Um, yeah."

He switched on a light. Her hand came up to shade her eyes. "Don't! I have a killer headache."

The light went off.

"Can I get you something for it?"

"I just need some peace and quiet." She put her head down again, hoping he'd get the message and leave. "Close the door on your way out."

The whoosh of the door. She sighed. Thank God, he was gone.

Then she heard footsteps. Damn it. She buried her face deeper in her folded arms, like a kid hiding under a blanket, thinking if she couldn't see the monster, the monster couldn't see her. "Nick, please, go away."

"No." She could feel his presence, detect the hint of aftershave he used. He stood beside her, then knelt down. "Kara told you everything, didn't she?"

"Please, Nick."

"I could see it in your face. Even J.J. knew something had happened."

Her head throbbed. "Yes, she told me. We'll talk about it later. I'll be fine if you'd just go."

No answer. Then a hand on her back. Rubbing, soothing. It broke the dam inside her. Sobs came, not a few tears, but major flooding.

She felt herself drawn up. Lifted out of the chair. Too raw to reject his comfort, to keep her distance, she clung to his neck. He moved, sat. She buried her face in his shoulder and let her agony pour out in huge racking sobs. Minutes later—she had no idea how many—she finally quieted and became aware of things. His gentle stroking. His words, "It's okay… It's okay…."

For a long time, she stayed where she was, in his arms, taking comfort from him. Finally she drew back and he switched on a small table lamp.

Nick's heart broke when he got a good look at Madelyn's face. He'd seen that expression only once before, when she'd first told him she'd been raped. He brushed back her hair, much as he'd done then, and wiped her cheeks with his thumbs. "I am so sorry you had to go through this."

"It worked, though, for Kara."

"At your expense."

"Small price to pay."

"I don't know about that."

"No, really, she told me everything."

"We'll discuss that in a minute. I'm concerned about you now."

She glanced around the office. It was as though she were trying to piece things together—where she was, what had happened. "I lost it. I was sitting at my desk, trying to keep what she told me in perspective, trying to separate her experience from mine. I couldn't do it."

"Of course you couldn't. We were both afraid this would happen if she opened up to you."

"Still, it took me by surprise."

"I wish it could have been different."

She stared at him a minute, then relaxed back against his chest. Her whole body deflated. "Just let me stay here a little while longer."

He encircled her with his arms and kissed her hair. "As long as you want, sweetheart."

"How's J.J.?"

He recognized her need to talk about something else. "Good question. He says the hit list was a ploy to scare the boys who bullied him."

"Do you believe him?"

"Something in my gut does."

"What will you tell Abby Franklin on Tuesday?"

"The truth. He agreed."

"Let me know if I can help."

"You're something, else, Maddie. I admire you so much. You're so strong. Resilient."

"I don't feel that way right now."

"Tell me what Kara said. Get all this out in one fell swoop."

In halting sentences, she recounted the details Kara had shared with her. Nick held her, he swore, his rage threatening to overwhelm him, especially when she confided that Kara had indeed been a virgin, as Maddie had expected.

When she finished, he asked, "What's she going to do now?"

"I didn't bring that up. It was too soon to discuss the next steps. She said I could tell you."

"That makes me feel better."

She sat up again. "Well, *this* made *me* feel better. You always make me feel better about what happened, Nick."

"You said that at the mall the day we found Kara in the bathroom." He brushed fingers down her cheek. "I'm glad." He wanted to say so much more. But he didn't.

He'd met a few times with Abe over the last week, but he didn't dare get his hopes—or Madelyn's—up before he made any real progress. He hadn't consciously decided to keep the counseling from her until he saw her break down today. She was a lot more fragile than she let on to other people.

Sliding off his lap, she stood. "I'm okay now," she repeated. "I'll go home, take a bath and relax in front of the TV."

He stood, too. "I'll drive you." He touched her hair again. "You look whipped."

"No, I'm fine. You were a big help, but really, I'm okay." Standing on tiptoes, she kissed his cheek.

He held her for a minute, but finally had to let her go.

She stepped around him to her desk.

Before he let himself persuade her to change her mind, he crossed to the door. "Good night, Maddie."

"Good night, Nick."

It was hell leaving her. But he intuitively recognized that being on her own was what she needed, and so he did what was best for her. Put her needs ahead of his own.

Maybe everybody was making progress in their therapy, himself included. With that thought, he quietly left Maddie alone with her ghosts.

CHAPTER TWELVE

OVER THE WEEKEND, Madelyn had a nightmare about Kara's rapist and hers; the two became one and prowled her dreams until they woke her. So, she told herself it was only because she hadn't slept much and because it had been a tough few days that she was disappointed when she awoke Tuesday morning and found she'd started her period. The last thing she needed was an unexpected pregnancy. Nick had panicked the last time, and his reaction wouldn't be any different now.

Maybe it would be.

Stop! she told herself. Intellectually, she knew nothing was different, even though he'd told her he loved her. Even though he'd gone to see his mother after D.C. But in the secret recesses of her heart, she couldn't help hoping those things indicated a desire to change. But the reality was he was still the same Nick. In so many ways, that was good. She loved everything about him except his inability to trust others.

She went through her morning routine, gathered her things and headed to her car. This was a positive development, she thought as she felt her stomach cramp. No complications. No mess.

Because the thought depressed her, she made herself focus on work. On Kara, primarily. She wanted to talk to Nick before her next private session with the girl. Madelyn had been in no condition to discuss Kara when he'd come to her office, but she'd seek him out today.

And while she was with him, she could tell him, *Oh, by the way, I'm not pregnant. You can rest easy.*

The Center was quiet at 7:00 a.m. The only cars in the lot were Nick's Eclipse and Abe's SUV. She entered the building and went down the hall to Abe's office. The door was closed. They both often came in early and sometimes she had coffee with him, chatted about her schedule for the day, listened to his. He was a skilled counselor and a nice man. Feeling the need for his soothing company, she rapped her knuckles on the wood. No response.

"Abe, it's me, Madelyn. Are you up for some coffee?"

A murmur of voices. Oh, dear, she hoped she hadn't interrupted. But there weren't other cars in the lot…and it was too early for clients. Was he with Nick? Maybe they were consulting on a case.

The door opened a crack. Abe stood in her line of vision so she couldn't see inside.

"I'm sorry. Are you busy?" she asked.

The older man's kind eyes were serious. "Yes. Only for another thirty minutes. Did you need something?"

"No. Just looking for a coffee buddy."

"Later?"

"You're on."

Madelyn walked down to her office. She was feeling really lousy. Her symptoms often worsened as the day progressed when she had her period. Once inside, she went to her desk, took some Advil from the drawer and swallowed it. She looked at the mess she'd left yesterday. Very unlike her. The surface was piled high with folders of what she needed to accomplish today. Francy had typed a schedule for her the night before and she picked it up. Suddenly, she felt overwhelmed.

The couch on the other side of the room beckoned. She'd feel better if she stretched out for a few minutes.

Lying down, she closed her eyes.

"Maddie?"

She stirred.

"Maddie?"

A weight next to her. Turning to her side, she buried her face in the cushion.

A hand on her shoulder. "Honey, are you all right?"

Nick. She grasped his thigh, pressed her face into it. She loved the way he smelled, so male and musky.

She heard a chuckle. "You'd better watch what you're doing, sweetheart. You're straying into dangerous territory. We're at work and it's ten o'clock in the morning."

Madelyn opened her eyes. "Ten o'clock?"

"Yes." His gaze became intense. "Are you okay?"

"Uh-huh. I came in early, but didn't feel well, so I decided to rest for a minute."

"More like two hours."

Her mind was foggy. "How do you know when I came in? I didn't see you."

His brows raised, and something drifted through his eyes. "Were you with Abe?"

He didn't answer immediately. "I guess I heard you arrive." He touched her stomach with gentle care. "You said you didn't feel well?"

She watched his hand resting on her middle. Heard the odd tone in his voice. "Don't worry, Nick. I'm not pregnant."

"You're not?"

"I got my period this morning. That's why I don't feel well."

His jaw tightened. "I see." She couldn't read his tone.

"You can breathe easy. You won't have to take off again."

He swallowed hard. "Well, I guess I deserve that."

"I'm sorry. I shouldn't have said that. I don't want to hurt you."

Staring out the window, he said, "I wish…" but didn't go further.

Madelyn waited, hoping he would, but when he didn't, she sat up. "I've got a lot to do today."

"Yeah, sure." He stood fast, like a kid who'd gotten a reprieve from the teacher's displeasure. "I'll let you get to it." Quickly, he left the room.

And that was that. If Madelyn had harbored any hope that he was ready to accept the possibility of a baby, she'd been badly mistaken. He couldn't wait to get out of there.

NICK HAD TO get out of there. He'd almost told her that instead of being relieved, he was disappointed she wasn't pregnant. He and Abe had been talking about the situation. As Abe's client, Nick had confided about what had happened between him and Madelyn. He'd shocked even himself when he'd confessed a part of him wished she were pregnant so that he and she would be forced to find a way to be together.

Since last Saturday at the parade, he'd seen Abe five times. He hadn't talked about what had happened to him on the streets, but the prospect of telling someone was nö longer terrifying. However, it was still too soon to let Maddie know about the counseling. He couldn't risk hurting her more in the end if he wasn't able to get past all the anger inside himself. That's why he hadn't stayed, why he'd left her alone.

He went to his office and had just sat down when his cell phone rang. Caller ID told him it was Dan.

"Hey," Nick said clicking on.

"Hi. How you doing?"

"Same old, same old."

"Huh. I was hoping not."

"What do you mean?"

"Saturday's Sara's birthday."

Thoughts of his niece and the MP3 player he'd gotten her made him smile. "I remember. There's a party planned. Where's it at again?"

"We're starting out at a local bowling alley. Then we're coming back here for cake, ice cream and a sleepover."

"A sleepover? Poor you."

"Sara made me promise to check and to see that you're coming to the bowling alley."

"Of course I am."

"She invited Mom, Nick."

"I can handle that."

A long hesitation. "And Dad."

Nick didn't know what to say. He waited for the familiar bitterness to rise up and consume him. But this time, he felt only empty.

Just then Madelyn walked past his doorway and down the hall. With her fleeting form in his mind, with Dan's admonition the other day to try to work on his relationship with Claire and Daniel, Nick said, "Tell Sara I'll be there. And Dan, don't worry."

He felt a bit light-headed when he hung up. He'd made a huge commitment. Abe's words echoed in his head. *Let's see if we can make even more progress.* This was a start, Nick guessed.

Checking the clock, he realized it was time to go to J.J.'s school. He picked up his keys and left his office. Madelyn was talking with Abe down the hall.

Nick called out, "I'm on my way to East High to see J.J.'s principal about his reinstatement."

"Good luck," Madelyn said with a small smile.

Abe gave him a thumbs-up.

As soon as he walked into the principal's office and saw that the superintendent was there, along with a woman he'd never met, Nick knew he was going to need all the luck he could get. There was a definite strain in the room. As a kid, he'd felt it often enough, in offices like this, whenever adults were about to make decisions for him.

"Hello," Abby Franklin said. She looked weary. "Nick Logan, this is Martine Como, the school's attorney. And you've met Superintendent Gray."

Nick greeted them. Before he could decipher exactly what was going on, J.J. and his aunt appeared at the door, escorted by the secretary who'd shown him in.

"Good morning, J.J. Mrs. Camp." Franklin's smile was forced. "Won't you sit down over here?"

Everyone took a chair at the conference table. The principal began. "J.J., this meeting was originally set up to decide what was going to happen to you for the rest of the year. We'd intended to wait for Mr. Logan's report and then make a plan for you until June."

"Yeah, I know." J.J. frowned. "You're talkin' like things have changed."

Franklin looked at the attorney.

She nodded.

Nick felt his spine prickle.

"After a lot of discussion, and much soul-searching, we've changed our minds about that. We've already made a plan for you."

Nick leaned forward. "Excuse me? You did all this without talking to me? Without waiting for a psych evaluation?"

The lawyer sat up straight and leveled Nick with a stare of authority. "Yes, we did. After I spoke with Ms. Franklin and Dr. Gray last week, I recommended that J.J. not be allowed back in school for the rest of the year."

J.J. gripped the edge of the table. "What? Why?"

Nick touched his arm. "Let's hear her out."

His eyes were wide and wild. "You said you'd help."

"I will. Give me a chance." He spoke directly to the principal, sensing she was sympathetic. "I think you can see how a unilateral decision like this will affect J.J. At least let me give you my evaluation."

"Of course we're interested in that; you can give us your professional opinion today. We'll also need a full written report. But it would be unfair of us to let you go on without telling you what we've already decided."

"I think you're being unfair by making a premature decision."

Franklin flushed. "I understand your feelings. And I assure you that this wasn't a decision that was easily reached." She nodded to the superintendent and the lawyer. "We've all agonized over it."

"What about me?" J.J. asked. "Doesn't anybody care about me and how I feel?"

"Of course we do, J.J. We'll discuss our reasons with you."

"Why are you doing this to me?" J.J.'s voice was like a child's. "*They* hurt *me*. They broke my freakin' arm and you let *them* back in."

"We don't consider them a threat to the school," Martine Como said. "We think you may be."

J.J. threw back his chair and stood. Nick got up and put a hand on the boy's shoulder but addressed the other adults in the room. "What if I don't agree? J.J. said he only meant to scare the kids who've been plaguing him all year, that what he wrote wasn't a hit list."

The principal shook her head. "Mr. Logan, we're not going to get into an argument with you. Our plan of action has already been decided. Truthfully, I hope what you say is true. Because when we consider J.J.'s placement for next year, we'll take that into consideration."

Nick felt J.J.'s shoulders tense under the thin material of his white T-shirt. "Next year? You mean I might have to go to another school *again?* I might not be able to come back here?"

Franklin raised her chin. "There's a strong possibility that another school will be better for you."

J.J.'s whole body went rigid. "This is bullshit." Tears welled in his eyes. "I didn't do anything."

Superintendent Gray spoke for the first time. "I'm afraid when you wrote that list, you did, indeed, do something, young man."

"Can we all sit down and see if we can come up with a better alternative?" Nick suggested. "We all want what's best for J.J."

Como frowned. "No, Mr. Logan, we cannot. As the legal representative for the school, I have to recommend we put the needs of the many over the needs of the few."

Nick shook his head. "That's a horrible thing to say in front of a child."

The woman held his gaze, but said no more.

Nick made eye contact with all three school officials. "Nobody's going to help us out here?"

Finally, Franklin said, "I'm sorry we have to be so blunt. But there's no sense in getting anybody's hopes up. Decisions have been made."

J.J. started for the door. "I'm outta here."

Nick yanked him back. "Not yet."

The boy shrugged Nick off. His expression turned cold. "I was right all along. Nobody can help me." He shot a venomous look at Ms. Franklin. "Thanks for nothing, lady." And he stormed out of the office.

His aunt, who'd been silent during the whole meeting, stared at them blankly. "What do I do now?" she asked. "I don't know what to do now."

"I'll help you figure that out," Nick said to the older woman. "We should go after him." He turned to the administrators. "Surely you can see this is a very bad decision for J.J."

"But it's best for the school," Principal Franklin added. "I'm sorry."

Nick shook his head. "Yeah, me, too. Let's go see what kind of damage control we can do, Mrs. Camp."

By the time they got outside, J.J. was nowhere in sight.

MADELYN SMILED at Kara, who sat before her in a powder-blue blouse and jeans. She looked young and innocent in the outfit and remarkably calmer than she had on Friday. Her parents had taken her out of town for a wedding on Saturday, so Madelyn hadn't met with her again. They'd talked once on the phone—Madelyn had called to see how she was— and exchanged a couple of e-mails before this session, but their contact had been light and casual and they hadn't dealt with anything heavy.

"How are you feeling today?" Madelyn asked.

"Better." She plucked at the hem of her blouse. "Confession must really be good for the soul."

"I'm not sure you had anything to *confess,* but getting stuff out does. It takes a lot of energy to keep a door closed when it's holding in so much baggage."

"I guess. It still hurts, but doesn't seem as bad. And I'm sleeping a lot better."

"All that's good, Kara."

"I'm glad you know. Did you tell Nick?"

"Yes. He had suspected, too, but he was still outraged for you."

She looked around the teen room. "I thought he'd be here today."

Madelyn glanced at her watch. "He was planning to be, but there was an emergency." He'd called to tell her the bad news about J.J. "He's been gone all day trying to help someone out." Right now he was over at J.J.'s house, but the boy hadn't gone home after the fiasco with the principal. Nick was waiting with J.J.'s aunt for him to show up. His tone of voice told her he was really worried. "I doubt he'll even make it back for the support group later."

"It's okay if Nick knows." Kara bit her lip. "Nobody else, though."

Madelyn hadn't planned on bringing this issue up in their very next meeting, but the opening was here. "Should we talk about that?"

"What do you mean?"

"For starters, I think you should tell your parents what happened to you."

"I can't do that."

"Why, honey?"

"It would hurt my mom too much. She's so sensitive and takes everything to heart. And my dad wouldn't want to hear it. Him and me don't talk about personal stuff."

"Kara, they're your parents, they would want to help." Briefly Madelyn thought about herself, having no mother to count on. And Nick having been kicked out of his home when he was younger than Kara. "They seem to me like people you can trust."

The girl's dark eyes widened under her brown bangs. "No. I won't do that."

"Kara, if you don't tell them, then it limits your options elsewhere."

Her expression turned panicky. "Elsewhere? What do you mean?"

Madelyn hesitated. "The school. The police." At Kara's pallor, she added, "Are you going to let Eric Zacko get away with this?"

"I don't want to talk about that."

"Because it's scary."

"Are you kidding? You don't know how scary. People will find out…he'll tell them I said yes. If you could see him…he's beautiful and I'm so ugly. Not even the adults would believe me. They'll say he wouldn't have to resort to…"

"Rape."

She swallowed hard. "They'll say I'm making it all up."

"Maybe. But the school and maybe even the police would have to conduct an official investigation. You'd get to tell your story. Eric Zacko would be questioned. I'd be asked my opinion. It wouldn't end in the front seat of his car."

Gripping the arms of the chair, Kara stared down. Shook her head. "You don't know. It was so awful. I could never talk about it in public."

"Yes, Kara, you could. I'd stay with you while you did it. Help you through it."

"No." She looked at Madelyn's face. "I went on the Internet. Rape isn't like other crimes. The victim's blamed."

"Sometimes. We have to work to change that in society. We have to start by reporting the crime."

"You don't know, Madelyn. You don't know."

Madelyn stared hard at the young girl. Her heart hurt for Kara and for herself. After a moment she said, "Yes, I *do* know."

Kara cocked her head.

"I do know what it's like to be raped. What it's like to testify in court. What it's like to face your accuser." Madelyn swallowed hard. "I especially know how much better you feel afterward.'

The young girl stilled. "How do you know?"

Starkly, Madelyn said, "Because I was raped, too."

NICK SPENT MOST of Tuesday trying to make contact with J.J. The boy had come home sometime during the night, after Nick had left his house. Mrs. Camp had called Nick today, Wednesday, because J.J. was holed up in the basement. But when Nick went over there, the cellar door was locked from the inside and J.J. refused to see or talk to him.

As an added concern, his aunt had mentioned to Nick that she might not be able to take care of J.J. anymore. He begged her to put a hold on any decisions now and especially not to say anything to J.J. about her fears. Nick didn't know how much more the boy could take.

By Wednesday night, Nick was exhausted. Wondering if he was doing anything worthwhile at the Center, he'd gone home about nine and taken a shower.

He'd slipped into jeans and was trying to remember when he'd last eaten when his doorbell rang.

J.J.? No, the kids didn't know where he lived. He'd given them his cell phone number and a couple of them had text messaged him, but he never gave out his address.

Madelyn? He doubted it. They'd been deliberately avoiding each other. He'd been devastated by his inability to help J.J., and by his own therapy with Abe, which—because he was close to a breakthrough—left him exposed. He was afraid of what he'd do if he sought Madelyn out. On her part, Madelyn was dealing with Kara's revelation and she didn't seem to want to talk to him about what she was feeling. Intuitively, they both understood that their vulnerability could make them forget that they shouldn't be together.

The bell rang again just before he pulled open the door.

Madelyn was on his stoop, dressed in yoga clothes—some yellow cropped pants and a yellow shirt to match. Stupidly, he said, "Did you go to yoga?"

"Yes. I was on my way home from the night class and I started driving to Beth's—" she looked around "—but I ended up here."

He wondered how she knew where he lived. "Come in."

"Were you…am I…" She took in his bare chest and feet, then looked past him and her eyes widened. "Is someone here?"

"No. I just got out of the shower. I went back over to J.J.'s after work and he wouldn't talk to me. His aunt is beside herself."

"I'm sorry."

"Come in."

He led her from the entrance up a flight of polished oak stairs to the living area.

"This is nice," she said. One huge room with windows overlooking the street, it had a kitchen at the other end.

"Thanks." He guided her by her elbow. "Come and sit."

They went to the big leather couch that faced the windows in the summer and would be turned around to face a fireplace on the adjacent wall in the winter. Madelyn dropped down on a cushion. Pushing back her hair, she sighed. "I don't know what to say."

"Tell me why you came. Something with Kara?"

"In a sense. Mostly me." She peered over at him and bit her lip. "I told her what happened to me, Nick."

"When?"

"Yesterday."

"You didn't mention it when I saw you today."

"You were so worried about J.J. And I thought I could handle this on my own." She shrugged and looked around. "I guess I couldn't. I know I shouldn't be here—this isn't helping…us—but I needed to come."

"Never mind that. Tell my why you told her."

"She was determined not to tell anybody else

except you that she'd been raped. I hadn't planned to deal with that issue so soon, but since she brought it up, I had no choice. So I tried to get her to think about confiding in her parents and then reporting the rape to the school and then the police. She kept saying I didn't understand what it was like."

"Was it hard revealing what happened to you?"

"Not as hard as hearing her story." She shook her head. "It was freeing, actually. I told you and Beth about the rape, but I think I was still keeping it a secret from everybody else. That's why I never wrote about it in the journal I shared with the kids or talked about it at the adult support group. Funny, isn't it? I kept assuring Kara she'd feel better not holding everything in, and it worked that way for me, too."

Gently, he placed his hand on her shoulder. When she didn't pull back, he slid it to her neck. Massaged her.

"Hmm. That feels good."

"What are you thinking?"

"Mostly, I'm questioning what I did with Kara. Telling her might have helped me, but she reacted badly. She was upset about being pushed to talk about this in public and she left the Center confused and a little angry at me, too."

"I'm sorry. That must have been hard."

"I've tried calling her a couple of times, but she won't answer my messages." Madelyn leaned closer to him. "Sometimes I don't think I'm doing anybody much good."

He kissed her hair. "I know the feeling."

"Why?"

"Are you kidding? I didn't exactly work miracles with J.J."

"You're great with him, Nick. I've watched you with all the kids. Progress is slow, and sometimes takes a while to manifest itself. But you're the best teen counselor I've ever met."

"All of that goes for you, Maddie."

She laughed. "We're a pair."

The camaraderie was familiar. The sharing of personal joys and worries about work was something they'd done in the past. And with it came an old intimacy that was equally familiar. And comforting. And thrilling at the same time.

"What do you need, Maddie?" he whispered. But he knew, by God.

She must have felt it, too, because she turned farther into him and slid her arms around his waist. "This."

"OH, GOD, YES, there."

"You are so beautiful. Here." He kissed her breasts. "Here." He went lower. "And here." Lower.

"Hmm. You make me believe I'm beautiful."

"You are."

"I…oh, Nick."

"Shh. Let it happen. Come for me, love."

"MADDIE, BABY, when did you become such a tease… Oh, wow."

"I love how your body swells beneath my hands."

"It's swelling, all right."

She kissed his breastbone. Tongued his nipples. "I'd forgotten how much fun this could be."

"In D.C. it was…arrgh…"

"Powerful. Sentimental. Meaningful. This is…"

"Hot!" He grasped her shoulders. "Stop teasing. Do it or let me come inside you."

"How can I lose?" she said kissing her way down his body.

SHE LAY WITH him on his bed, naked in the moonlight that streamed in through gauzy blinds. Her back to his torso, she settled into him. "Thanks, for this."

He kissed her hair. "My pleasure."

"I knew it was dangerous coming over here. But I couldn't stop myself, Nick. I was too drained."

"I know. My resistance was zilch, too. Let's not analyze it to death, though."

"Okay."

"Go to sleep."

"I haven't been sleeping much." As if on cue, she yawned.

He positioned her more comfortably. "Me, either."

"Close your eyes. It's midnight. Relax. We'll talk in the morning."

Midnight

Checklist:

4 Pyrex containers

Mixing bowls
Hydrometer
Bleach
Potassium chloride
Igniters
Timers
Diagram from the Internet: Making Plastic
Explosives from Bleach

IN THE BASEMENT of his aunt's house, J.J. checked his watch. Just enough time. He only needed one more thing. His aunt had kept his father's belongings for him down here. She didn't know all the contents of the cartons. He got up from the work table, opened some boxes, rummaged around and found what he was looking for.

Mentally, he added to the list:

Shotgun.

Shells.

Grabbing the items, he set them on the table and began the assembly. Hours later, before his aunt got up, J.J. climbed the stairs with his paraphernalia and headed out the back door. For a minute, he felt bad. It had been okay living here. His aunt had been nice to him for the most part.

Then he remembered: *I'm sorry, J.J., you're too much to handle. I can't do it anymore. I called Social Services today. They're coming out tomorrow to talk about what to do.*

Nobody wanted him. They'd put him in the system and he'd rot there. He'd seen specials on TV about what happened to kids like him in foster care and group homes.

Not in this lifetime!

CHAPTER THIRTEEN

HER STOMACH jumping like a pond of frogs, Kara rushed to the bathroom on Thursday morning as the first period bell rang. In a stall, she thought she might puke, but she didn't. Instead, she sat down and buried her face in her hands. Madelyn's words from Tuesday haunted her....

It won't end in the front seat of his car....

You should tell your parents....

I was raped, too...I know what it's like to face your accuser....

No wonder Kara had felt close to the woman from the beginning. But now, Madelyn wanted her to do something she just couldn't do. The counselor had called her several times, but Kara had been too much of a coward to talk to her. And it made her sick to her stomach.

She heard the giggles of girls entering the bathroom.

"I hate math. Lincoln the Lush smells even more funky today. Must be he had a bad night."

"I'm out of gym. Lied about my period."

Quickly Kara raised her feet and braced them on the door. She didn't want to face the cheerleaders, whose identity she recognized from the voices.

"Freak! I got mine for real." That one was Melanie Hanks, Eric Zacko's girlfriend.

"Lucky you that you got it," another said. Amber Lewis, Mel's best friend. "After what happened."

Melanie sniffled. "The scumbag." Then Kara heard crying. The tears sounded real, though these girls could trick teachers and administrators alike with their phony outbursts.

"Aw, Mel, don't cry, he isn't worth it." Suzette, the most popular, and the cruelest, spoke with authority. Kara had seen her decimate girls her age and even some of the new teachers.

Kara could picture them out there. Fluffing their streaked hair. Applying lipstick. Spritzing on expensive perfume. She'd seen them perform the routine several times. They always talked like this, too, even if she was at a sink, or coming out of a stall. Like she was invisible.

To them, she was.

"I hate him!" Melanie again. "He told me he *stopped*."

Amber swore lewdly. "Old E.Z. does it again. Hell, how many notches on his belt does he need?"

E.Z. That's what the guys called Eric. Kara had never thought about why. E.Z. as in *easy*. Oh, God.

"Who's it this time?" Amber asked.

"Sara Langdon."

"The mousy one in our social studies class?" Suzette sounded disgusted. "I think I copied her test once."

"Jeez, he stays true to type." Amber sounded disgusted, too.

"I don't get it," Melanie whined. "I do whatever he wants because he's my boyfriend. Why do those girls do it? What's in it for them?"

Bile rose in Kara's throat. *Them.* The pieces of the horrible puzzle began to fall into place.

"Makes them feel important, I guess." Kara could hear Amber snap her gum. "But, hell, what's this, his fourth?"

His *fourth?*

"I told him after the last time we were done if he did it again."

The *last* time?

"Good for you," Amber said. "It sucks."

A chuckle from one of them. "No, they do."

Mean girl laughter bounced off the walls of the lav, found its way into the stall and pierced Kara's heart.

A teacher's voice intruded. "What's going on in here?"

"Oh, nothing, Ms. Michaels," Suzette said sweetly.

"Are all of you out of class?"

"Um, yeah."

"Funny, huh? An emergency at the same time." Ms. Michaels's tone was sarcastic. "Come on, I'll escort you back to your classes. See what your teachers think of this little sorority meeting."

They left, begging the English teacher not to report them.

Kara dropped her feet to the floor. She felt light-headed. *Put your head between your knees, honey.* Just thinking about Madelyn's voice calmed her.

And instead of falling apart, Kara felt something else swell inside her.

It took her a minute to recognize the emotion.

Outrage.

BAREFOOT, wearing one of Nick's shirts, Madelyn was whisking eggs and humming to herself when he came into the kitchen. Sun streamed in through the window and felt warm on her face. "That's good to hear."

Her back still to him, she smiled to herself. "I feel…good."

Arms slid around her waist. "You do." He nosed her hair. "You smell good, too." So did he, of just-applied aftershave.

"I used your shampoo."

"No, babe. I used my shampoo. On you. And my soap. Other places." He punctuated the phrases with kisses on her neck and shoulders.

She chuckled. "I remember."

"Hmm." He stepped back and, at the counter next to her, poured coffee. This morning he could be an ad for…anything…in a magazine. He wore jeans, no shirt and was barefoot, too. His dark hair was damp and wavy. "I can't believe we slept this late." It was eight o'clock when they woke up. Nine by the time they'd showered and made love in the stall.

"I'll clear it with your boss." Madelyn's tone was dry.

He laughed and dropped down at the table. "I didn't have anything scheduled till noon."

"My first appointment's at eleven."

"I should check my messages, though."

"Me, too." Reaching over, she fished her phone out of her purse on the counter and turned it on. "Responsibility. Sometimes I hate being an adult."

"I know the feeling." His phone chimes rang. "There's a text message." He fiddled with the buttons.

"I've got a voice mail." The cell to her ear, Madelyn clicked in.

"Madelyn, this is Kara. It's Thursday morning. I'm at the Center. I need to talk to you. Something's happened. Where are you? Please call me. Now. This can't wait."

"I have a message from Kara." She said the words aloud and then looked over at Nick.

His face was white as he stood and he threw back the chair.

"What is it?"

"My text message is from Carla Santos. She's in first period gym class at East High School, and said J.J.'s got the class held hostage there."

"Hostage?"

He was getting his keys from the cupboard. "He's got a shotgun. And there are bombs in the gym."

"Oh, dear Lord." She turned off the stove. "I'm coming with you." She glanced at her phone. "Damn, Kara said she needed to see me now."

"You should go talk to her." He grabbed a shirt off the chair and slipped into sandals. "No telling what's happened. I'll go to the school."

Her heart beat fast. "All right. I'll come over as soon as I can."

Nick headed for the door.

She called out, "Nick, be careful."

"I will." He came back in and kissed her nose. "I love you."

He was gone before she realized she hadn't said *I love you* back. Had never, ever, said the words to him.

Shotgun.

Bomb.

School.

Columbine.

Oh, God. Would she have another chance?

IT WAS LIKE a scene out of a movie, complete with a messy drizzle, which had just started. Nick pulled up to East High School's entrance, where a police roadblock had been set up. Hundreds of students had been herded to the bus garage parking lot, while lights flashed and cops milled around. Voices echoing through bullhorns, shouts and an occasional siren filled the air.

A police officer, looking harried and irritated, walked over to him. "I'm sorry, sir, you can't go in here. If you're a parent, your child is probably in the parking lot over there."

Not if he was in gym class. "I'm not a parent, I'm a counselor for the Rockford Crime Victims Center."

The cop gave him a *"so?"* look.

"I'm the boy's counselor, the boy with the bombs."

Startled at first, the police officer's expression turned to one of disgust. He didn't have to say anything to make his feelings known. Some counselor, huh? He gestured for Nick to park on the side of the access road which led to the bus garage, the administration building and the high school.

Nick got out of his car and spotted Sam across the way. "Sergeant Delaney can clear me. Sam," he yelled to her.

Sam saw him and strode over. Her expression was worried. "Nick, I just tried to call you. How did you know to come?"

"Carla Santos text messaged me." He swallowed hard. "She and Hector are in the gym class J.J.'s holding hostage."

"Oh, no."

He gave her what details he had.

"That helps. We've had to piece together what's going on in there. Another kid had his cell phone with him, but most of them didn't because they were in gym class. Anyway, the boy called his parents. It looks like J.J. got in to school before everybody else, planted some bombs in the gym, then hid and waited for first period to begin. When the kids and teachers came into the gym area, he made himself known. Besides the bombs in the gym, he's got one strapped around himself and he's carrying a gun. The boy talking on his cell got cut off in the middle of the call. J.J. probably found him on the phone."

"This is a real nightmare."

"We went into the school, but the doors to the gymnasium are secured from the inside. We tried talking to J.J., but he threatened to start shooting the students if we didn't go away."

"Damn it."

"At least the administrators got the other students out of the building."

"How many kids are still inside?"

"Around forty. Two classes were in the gym and two teachers."

Nick shook his head. "J.J. hated gym class. And he said the teachers did nothing to stop the bullying."

"Must be why he chose this particular class."

"What's the plan?"

"They've called in the bomb squad. And a SWAT team is on its way." She shook her head. "They'll try to get a clear shot on J.J. from the gym windows or the hallway in school, Nick, if somebody doesn't do something beforehand. After Columbine and all the more recent shootings, officials won't wait around to see what happens."

"Son of a bitch."

Over her shoulder, he saw Superintendent Gray and

Abby Franklin approach. When Gray reached them, he said, "What do you have to say now, Logan? Still believe Camp should have been let back into school?"

Sam said, "Maybe if he had been, this wouldn't have happened."

Abby Franklin looked to Nick. Her expression was sad. "Do you think the suspension brought this on?"

"In part." He explained what had happened with Mrs. Camp, a chain of events directly set into motion by J.J.'s suspension.

Franklin faced Sam. "Is there anything that can be done, Sergeant Delaney? Besides calling in snipers?"

Sam asked Nick, "Got any ideas?"

"Yes. Can you get me in there?"

J.J. FELT THE weight of the bomb strapped around his waist. Mentally he ticked off where he'd put the others: two in the far corners of the gym, and one under the bleachers. Four ought to do it. He'd followed the directions from the Internet site to the letter when he'd built them early this morning in his basement. And the timers on the bombs *should* work. He'd patterned them after the ones the London subway bombers used. They could only be set for an hour's delay to detonation time, but that was enough. Once he got everybody under control, he went around and started the timers. If by chance they didn't go off, he had the device around his waist and the shotgun. If the other bombs exploded like they should, he wouldn't be around to care.

He glanced across the gym and laughed, his head light, his mind spinning. Look at them now, all cowering on the bleachers like little boys afraid of the dark. Somebody said something and he lifted the weapon. Images of Eric Smith and Dylan Klebold brandishing shotguns ran through his mind. "Next person that says a word gets the first bullet."

He wondered if he'd have the balls to shoot one of them. Blowing everybody up in a puff of smoke was one thing. Shooting somebody at close range was different. He'd set the bombs on a timer to make the students sweat, especially the three jocks in the back row with their heads down, pretending to pray. It was no good unless they suffered before they died. They'd made him suffer enough!

Nobody was getting in here, either. He'd chained all the gym doors during the night. The other kids had gotten out; he'd heard the PA sounding the alarm and the voice of the principal calling for evacuation, then the thundering of hundreds of pairs of feet trying to escape. From him. It gave him a feeling of real power. At first, the cops had used bullhorns from the hall to try to talk to him. Until he threatened to start shooting the students.

He heard pounding on the door to the boys' locker room. Shit, there was no lock on the gym side for that one. He wondered who was stupid enough to try to come in here. He raised the shotgun and pointed it toward the entrance, ready to shoot whoever entered. The door creaked open. A man stepped into the gym.

Nick Logan.

J.J. swore vilely as Nick crossed to him.

"Hello, J.J."

The gun wobbled in his hand. "What are you doing here?" This was wrong. Somebody he liked wasn't supposed to be here. And why the hell would Nick put himself in danger?

"I've come to help you."

"Been there, done that. Didn't work." When Nick took another step, J.J. raised the gun higher. "Stay where you are." He yelled to the teacher sitting on the first row bench. "Hey, Nose. Slide the basket of balls over to the locker room door." He'd had them close off the divider to the other half of the gym already, so access could only come from this side.

"J.J.," Nick said quietly. "You don't want to do this."

"Yeah, I do."

"Why?"

"Shut up. I don't want to talk about it."

"I know you're upset about what your aunt told you."

"I said shut up."

"This problem can be fixed. Any problem can."

"Keep quiet or I'll shoot you."

"I don't believe that."

He cocked the gun. Stared at the man.

The man who'd tried to prevent his suspension…

I think you can see how a unilateral decision like this will affect J.J. At least hear me out on my evaluation…You're being unfair…J.J. said he only meant to scare the boys who've been plaguing him all year.

But in the end, Nick Logan was just another adult who'd failed to help J.J. Like everybody else. Why did he keep talking?

"I said stop."

When he didn't, J.J. pulled the trigger.

MADELYN'S HANDS were shaking as she opened her office door and found Kara sitting inside on the couch. She'd listened to the radio on the way to the Center. Most of the student body and staff had vacated the high school. Police, the bomb squad and SWAT teams were on the scene.

And Nick had walked into the melee.

"Hi, Madelyn," the girl said. "Sorry for making you come…" Kara stood. "What's wrong?"

"Nothing, honey. I'm glad you're here."

"You're lying."

Footsteps in the hall. John Kramer halted abruptly in the doorway. "Maddie, thank God you're in. Have you seen the news?"

"What news?" Kara asked.

John startled when he saw Kara. "I'm sorry. I didn't see your young friend."

"I was just going to tell her. Kara, there's been an incident. J.J. Camp has taken a gym class in his high school hostage."

"What?"

Quickly Madelyn explained the situation.

"And Nick's there?"

"Yes."

"We've got it on TV in the conference room," John told them.

"Come on," Kara said heading to the door. "I didn't know anything about this or I wouldn't have come over. What I have to say can wait."

They hurried out of the office and to the conference room. The staff was assembled there. Stone-faced, they were staring at the anchor on TV. No one spoke.

"This just in," a woman in a white blouse with perfectly coiffed hair said from the TV screen. "Shots have been fired in the gymnasium of East High School. I repeat, shots have been fired. No word from J. J. Camp, the boy who's holding the other students hostage. We do know a counselor from the Rockford Crime Victims Center entered the building minutes before the shot rang out."

"Nick," Madelyn whispered.

Beth got up and came to her side. Deanna crossed to Kara, took her hand and led her to a chair. Beth didn't speak, but slid an arm around Maddie.

Madelyn closed her eyes, wondering if Nick was still alive.

NICK SAT ON the bottom bleacher, staring at the holes J.J.'s shotgun had put in the padded wall at the far end of the gym. Either the boy was a lousy shot or he hadn't wanted to kill Nick. J.J. was across the room, calmer now, leaning against the partition, looking thin and frail and white as a ghost in a ripped T-shirt and jeans. He was watching the crowd of students huddled on the bleachers.

In that crowd Nick had spotted Carla and Hector. And a lot of jocks. He'd bet some of the bullies were among them.

Nick waited a few minutes, then stood and crossed to J.J.

"I told you to sit down." But J.J.'s tone lacked conviction.

He took it as a cue. "You don't want to shoot me, J.J., or you would have done it a few minutes ago."

"I don't want to, but I will." His voice quivered.

Nick hoped like hell he was reading the signs right. "I don't think so. Tell me what you're trying to do here, J.J.?"

"Blow this place off the map." He used several four letter words for emphasis.

"And all those innocent kids over there?"

"Are not so innocent."

"No? Most of them are."

"Some of them hurt me." The hand holding the gun shook. The other hovered near the red wire at his chest. "One of them broke my arm."

"J.J., look carefully at the group. On the left side. Halfway up."

J.J. scowled. "Is this a trick?"

"No, just look."

"It won't work to try to get the gun away. I'll pull the wire on the bomb and we'll go up in pieces."

"I know. I'm not going to try to get the gun. I swear I won't." He shook his head. "Look where I said."

J.J. looked. "Shit."

"Not so good, is it?"

"What are they doin' here?"

"Carla and Hector are in one of these gym classes. The coed one."

"I forgot about them. But now I remember, that day at the track."

"Yeah? Remember how nice they were to you at the march? Hector walked the whole way with you."

"He's okay."

"And Carla's always been kind."

J.J. watched them for a long time. Then he turned to Nick. His eyes were flat. "What was it she said?"

"Who?"

"That lawyer lady."

Nick choked back his anger. "I don't recall."

"I do. She said, 'The good of the many has to be put before the good of the few.'"

"WE HAVE A spokesperson for the Rockford Police Department live at headquarters to give us an update. We'll switch over to there now."

"No," Madelyn said aloud. "Don't leave the school."

The scene shifted to a somber-faced man with a reporter. He did not appear happy at being interviewed. "Erin Early here at the RPD talking with Detective

Sanchez. Detective, can you tell us what the options of the police and SWAT teams are at this point?"

"I'm afraid I can't."

"Rumor has it, snipers are in place to take out the student. But he has a bomb strapped to him."

"A bomb *strapped* to him? No." Maddie bit her lip. That meant J.J. planned to die, too. It made him a hundred times more dangerous. And Nick was in there with him. *Shots have been fired.* If he wasn't already dead.

"I'm afraid I can't go into our strategy." Sanchez scowled. "Just know that the Rockford law enforcement is on top of this."

"How long will you wait to take action?"

"Hard to tell. I will say the sooner something's done, the better."

"Did you give your approval for the counselor to go in? The one from the RCVC?"

"That I can confirm."

"Do you think it will help the situation? It's obvious counselors haven't been very effective with the boy so far."

"I hope so."

"Um, hello."

Madelyn turned at the sound of a voice behind her. In the doorway of the conference room was Dan Logan. His face devoid of color, he gripped the doorjamb. "I—I didn't know…I know I can't help here, but I…Tessa's on an overnight field trip with Molly…so I came here."

Madelyn watched him for a moment, then crossed the room and hugged Nick's brother.

"Is it as bad as it sounds?" he asked, holding her tightly.

"I'm afraid so." She drew back and took his hand. "Come and wait with us."

J.J.'S HEAD STARTED to pound like drumbeats. It was because he hadn't slept in thirty-six hours. Not because Hector and Carla had come up to him and were standing in front of Nick. The three of them weren't supposed to *be* here.

"J.J., what are you doing?" Carla asked.

"I'm not gonna talk to you."

"You don't wanna hurt anybody from our group, do you? Remember what we all said at the march? That we'd stick together."

J.J. remembered that. He also remembered Carla standing up to Cougar and Hector coming over with his friends to help. Over their shoulders, he saw Cougar, with the rest of the jocks, watching him. "I know all that. But I can't let you go."

"Yes, you can," Nick put in. "You can let everybody go. It isn't too late."

"It is." He pointed to the bomb. "I'm toast either way."

Nick shook his head. "No, you're not. If you don't hurt anyone, you can still have a future."

"You don't know what you're talkin' about."

"Yes, he does, J.J." Carla's voice was shaky.

"Dude, you gotta rethink," Hector said.

They didn't understand. "Look, I'd let you guys go if I could, but there's men outside these doors. We open one of them, they'll rush me." *Or shoot me.*

"Then you have to put down the gun, take off the bomb and tell us where the others are." Nick sounded so sure. "We can call out on my cell phone so they'll know what's going on and they won't hurt you."

"Don't you see? I can't. Even if I wanted to. It's too late."

"Of course you can." Nick again. "It will only be too late if you hurt somebody."

"They hurt me!"

"And they were wrong." Nick stepped up and put his hands on Carla's and Hector's shoulders.

"Get back. Don't come so close."

"I know what it's like, J.J., to lose everything. To lose a person you love, to lose your *home.*"

J.J. knew that. Nick had told him. "But you didn't do anything like this."

"No, but what you've done so far can be undone. You still have a chance."

Spots swam before his eyes. He felt himself sweating through his clothes. And suddenly he was so tired he could barely keep his eyes open.

"Please, J.J., do it for us." Carla had tears in her eyes.

"*Por favor, mi amigo.*" Hector—big macho Hector—looked scared shitless.

"J.J., listen to them. The three of us care about you. So do a lot of other people—Madelyn, the kids in the support group. We'll all help."

"I told you. Nobody can help."

"Yes," Nick said firmly,"we can."

MADELYN SAT next to Dan in chairs off to the side staring at the TV. The screen had switched back to the school, where officials were speculating about what was going to happen. "Outcomes in these situations are rarely good. Think of the school shootings in Columbine, Florida, New York City. The Amish girls in P.A."

Unable to listen to their line of conversation, Madelyn got up and crossed to the coffeepot, where she stood staring at it. She felt a presence behind her. "Maddie?"

Tears clouded her eyes. She turned. "Your brother calls me that."

"I know. He told us all about you."

"Yes, I gathered." She nodded to the TV. "I...I should have told him."

"What?"

"That I loved him." She searched Dan's face. His eyes were so like Nick's it made her tears overflow. "I had the chance this morning, and I didn't take it."

He took her hands and held them gently in his. "You'll have another chance."

"Will I?"

"Yes, we have to believe that."

"Why are we so stupid sometimes? Why do we think there will always be time to do what we should do?"

"I—"

Their attention was caught by a shriek from the TV.

"Oh, my God, look." This from the newscaster, who'd been perfectly calm up till now.

Madelyn and Dan looked.

On the screen was the gym side of the school. The air was still misty from the light rain, but eerily, the sun was peaking out and hitting the building. The camera zeroed in on the double entrance doors. They'd opened. Suddenly kids came running out. Madelyn saw Carla and Hector Santos among the group hurrying into the light. Others followed, single file and in clusters.

The newscaster's voice-over indicated she'd regained her composure. "As our footage shows, the students have been freed. No official word on the bomber. Or the shots we heard."

"I wonder what happened." This from her coanchor.

"Could we possibly get out of this without anyone being harmed?"

"It would take a miracle."

As the last kid raced out, it hit Madelyn that maybe not all the bombs had been deactivated. Otherwise why was everyone running like this?

Even the gym teachers came at a fast jog.

But no one else followed. The door closed with a thud and Madelyn felt her heart clutch so hard in her chest she put a hand over it. "Get out of there, Nick," she whispered. "Please…"

Then the door opened again and the SWAT team filed out. A man wearing a black jacket with Bomb Squad on it was next; he carried a metal box.

The last helmeted guy had J.J. by the upper left arm. His hands were cuffed behind his back.

And on his right was Nick. Alive. Safe.

The announcer said, "Well, there's the miracle worker, I guess. Nick Logan, the Rockford Crime Victims Center counselor."

Maddie dropped to the nearest chair, buried her face in her hands and began to sob.

CHAPTER FOURTEEN

ONCE AGAIN, Nick pulled up to the white clapboard house in Pittsford. Once again, he sat inside his car, staring at the small structure. This time, though, he knew he had to go through with what he'd planned. If he was to have a chance with Maddie, he had no choice.

He'd talked to her only briefly since the incident yesterday with J.J....

"I'm fine, sweetheart."

She'd burst into tears.

"Shh. I am."

"I..." Hiccups. "I know."

"I'm going to be tied up here, I think through the night."

"I understand. I need to talk to you when you have the chance."

"Me, too, to you. But not on the phone." He had a lot of things to say to Maddie, but he had to say them in person.

He glanced at the house again. He'd go in. In a minute. He needed to get ready. Hitching the seat

back, he stretched out his legs and closed his eyes.
He'd been up all night…

"I'm going to the station house with J.J.," he'd
said to the cops who'd taken the boy from the SWAT
team. Once J.J. surrendered the gun to Nick, the
bombs had been deactivated. They'd come out of the
building and made their way to the nest of cars that
had pulled up to the school.

"Not protocol," an RPD officer said. They were all
standing at a black-and-white.

J.J. had said nothing since he'd given Nick the
shotgun and taken off the bomb at his waist. Now his
eyes sparked to life. "You promised," he said to Nick.

"I know. And I mean to keep it."

Sam had hurried over to them. Nick explained he
situation. "Damien, if it weren't for Nick, the school
wouldn't be standing there anymore and nearly fifty
people would be dead."

Damien looked torn.

Sam said, "He can ride with me. You guys take J.J."

And so J.J. had been put in the backseat of the squad
car and Nick had ridden to the police station with Sam.
On the drive over, she'd outlined for him what would
happen next and vowed she'd get him in to see the boy.

Nick waited in the reception area on a bench until
J.J. was booked and put into a cell. True to her word,
Sam used her influence, and Nick was shown into the
holding area. Where he was catapulted into the past
and hit by a wave of anxiety that he hadn't expected.
He hated police stations. Bad things had happened

to him in them. Once, at about J.J.'s age, he'd been arrested and had been held in a cell until his mother could get him released. She'd fallen apart and made him feel like scum.

And she'd said he was just like his father....

He looked at her house. It was time to try to let go of all that. Get out of the car. Go inside. He glanced at the dash. Ten o'clock. If he drew this out, he'd miss the Friday noon support group at the Center. He wouldn't have to bare his soul. But he wasn't going to duck out of this session. He didn't want to.

So he opened the door and got out of the car. It had rained during the night and early morning, but the sun was shining now. He laughed as he took in the horizon. Arching over Claire's house was a rainbow. He raised his eyes to the heavens. "Thanks for the sign." His steps were lighter as he crossed the road.

He strode up the walkway, and when he reached the corner of the house, he heard noise coming from around back. Voices. She was outside. With someone. Probably Daniel. Nick remembered how he'd chickened out the last time he'd found his parents together. A door slammed.

Well, you're done with that, Nicky boy. If you can face down a bomb, you can do this.

Thinking about Maddie, he followed the redbrick path around the house.

Claire was standing with her back to him, staring out at the yard. She wore an ice-blue robe—her favorite color—and she was holding a mug of coffee. Colorful flowers surrounded the patio and bloomed in a garden beyond the house.

Nick swallowed hard. Stared at her hard. Then he said softly, "Mom?"

The cup clattered to the ground and shattered into pieces. Claire whirled around.

"I didn't mean to startle you."

"Nicolas?"

He glanced at the broken cup. "I know, it's a surprise."

"You called me..." Tears welled in her eyes and she put her hand to her mouth.

"Mom. I called you *Mom*." He felt like a little boy again, hopeful, wanting to please this woman.

She shocked him by rushing over and throwing herself at him. "Nicky."

He felt his eyes sting as he hugged his mother for the first time in over twenty years.

"I was so worried." She shook. Literally. After a long time, she drew back. Her eyes were awash with tears. "I watched on the TV. What you did. I was so afraid. And I vowed... Nicky, we have to make this right between us."

"I know we do."

"Please give me another..." A look of surprise. "You know?"

"Yes."

"Oh, thank God." She hugged him again.

"What's going on out here?"

Claire stiffened in his embrace. Nick knew why. She was remembering what had happened the last time he'd come to see her. He squeezed her arms, then drew back and circled around her. Slowly, he crossed the patio until he was standing in front of his father. They were about the same height, only Daniel carried more weight than he did. His eyes were also blue. And wide, now. They flickered with determination. He'd probably made some vows of his own yesterday.

For a minute, Nick felt the anger and resentment battering to get out. But as he looked at his father, all his rage seemed to dissipate.

Then, he reached out his hand and nodded his head. "Hello, Dad."

"I ORDERED OUT for lunch," Madelyn said to John as she set down the last of the bags she'd taken from the deliveryman. People were filing into the conference room for their regular Friday support group at noon. "I—I couldn't get it together to cook."

"I can imagine why." John patted her arm. "After the day we had yesterday, anything will do."

Although crime victim workers were a resilient bunch, yesterday's ordeal had taken a toll on all of them. When Nick and J.J. had finally appeared on the TV unharmed, some of the staff had been too stunned to move. Some, like Madelyn, had burst into tears. Then, Beth had gathered everyone around the table for a prayer of thanks. They watched the aftermath for a while, but eventually things had returned to normal and everyone had gone about their business. All day long, though, they were subdued and had stopped into Madelyn's office often for updates on Nick.

Kara had known, of course, that Maddie was still upset...

"I know you're tired and that the worry was awful."

"I'm better now. We can talk, honey." They were walking down the hall to her office. They went inside and Kara took a seat on the couch. Madelyn followed suit.

Kara said, "I'll talk. You listen. For a few minutes. And you don't have to take care of me."

Madelyn had been surprised. "Okay."

"I've decided to report Eric Zacko."

"I'm glad, Kara. What brought this on?" Madelyn studied the girl. "The thing with Nick and J.J.?"

But Kara had shaken her head. "No, that reinforced it, though. Made me feel stronger about doing this. But it was something else."

Kara had launched into a bizarre tale about how Eric Zacko preyed on unpopular, plain girls like her. Sweet-talking them. Seducing them. "And maybe even raping them, Madelyn. Like me."

"This is horrible."

"I'm going to tell my mother first, like you said. But I want you to come with us to the school. And maybe then to the police. If you can. I know you're upset about Nick. So I could do it alone, well, Mom and me, if I have to."

"No, I'll come. I *want* to come. I am so proud of you, honey."

"Yeah, well, it's bad enough he did this me. But those others? And maybe more? No way."

And so the process had begun. By three on Thursday afternoon, Kara had told her story to the principal, who didn't discount her version of the events, as Kara had feared, but questioned her fully. He'd called in all the counselors and asked if they knew anything about Eric Zacko's reputation. Some of them had heard rumors and had worked with a couple of girls he'd seduced. There were no reports of forced sex, though the principal was wise enough to realize how little that meant.

Through the whole thing, Kara remained calm and resolute. Madelyn couldn't have been more pleased and could hardly wait to tell Nick.

When the food was out, people began serving themselves. Madelyn drew a cup of coffee and stood off to the side, watching them.

"Maddie, aren't you eating?" Beth had come up to her.

"Not yet."

"Try to have something."

"Yes, Mom."

Beth squeezed her arm. "It's over, sweetie."

"I know. I'm just glad he's all right."

"Think he'll be here today?"

"No. Some people will do anything to get out of this support group, I guess."

Beth chuckled.

"Actually, I excused him. He called as soon as he could and then again last night. He said he'd try to make it into work today. I told him he deserved a day off."

"When will you see him?"

"As soon as I can. I have a lot to say."

"I'm sure you do." She waved her hand to encompass the rest of the people in the room. "Everybody showed up. I think yesterday sobered us all."

"Yeah, tragedy does that. Even near-tragedy."

After the staff ate, Madelyn sat down at the conference table. This was about the last thing she wanted to do—she *wanted* to see Nick—but duty called. "Well," she said dryly. "I think we can pretty much all agree on what the professional success of the Center was this week."

"Yeah," Joe said, "anything else will pale in comparison."

"Shall we share some personal things?" Beth suggested. "We could talk about what we're feeling today, after what happened with Nick and J.J. yesterday. These things have a tendency to help put our lives in perspective."

"I like that idea." Maddie smiled. "Who wants to go first?"

"I do."

All turned to the doorway. Nick stood there. He was leaning on the jamb, his hair messy, his beard stubbled around his jaw, the jeans and shirt that he'd had on yesterday morning, wrinkled. He looked tired and weary but so good Madelyn's pulse began to beat wildly at the sight of him, safe and here, where he belonged.

John got up first. He drew Nick inside the room and hugged him. "I was so worried, son."

Closing his eyes, Nick held on extra long. "I'm sorry you had to go through this, John. Was Lucy all right?"

John nodded.

They took turns. Deanna, Sam, Beth and Francy all hugged Nick.

Abe knocked fists with him and grinned. "Quite a show there, guy."

Joe rose, shook his hand and said, "Give you a lot of credit, Nick. I don't know if I could have done what you did."

From the table, Connor waved, and Nick said to him, "Thanks for coming down to the station house last night. You helped a lot."

Connor just shrugged.

Madelyn stayed where she was, watching the scene unfold.

Nick hadn't looked at Maddie yet. He was afraid of what he'd do if he did. Instead, he smiled at everybody, said a few words to each of them, then when they took their seats, Nick dropped down in the vacant chair at the other end of the table from her. Finally, he met her gaze. A slow smile spread across her face, and he matched it. "Hello, Maddie."

"Nick."

He addressed the group. "Everybody's calling me a hero today. The police. The press. Even some of you. But I want you to know, I'm not a hero. I'm the biggest coward alive."

People cocked their heads to listen. Some frowned.

"Nick, if you were scared when you walked into that gym yesterday, that doesn't mean you're a coward." John touched his arm. "Courage is proceeding when you *are* scared."

Briefly, he squeezed John's hand. "I know that. I wasn't referring to yesterday." He looked at Maddie again and took a deep breath. Damned if he wasn't going to do this right. "Some of you don't know what I'm referring to. But I'm gonna tell you. In public. In this setting." *Even if it kills me.* "Five years ago when I came to the Center, I fell in love with Madelyn." The room became very quiet. "It took me a whole year to get her to date me, but as a few of you know, she did. And then we spent the most wonderful thirteen months of my life together."

She smiled so sweetly at him, it gave him courage. "Nick, you—"

"Hush."

Again he looked away from her, and scanned all of them around the table. Abe nodded his encouragement. "What you all don't know is that I panicked. Actually it was like hitting a brick wall, head on, when I realized how dependent I was on her. And that she could leave me. I let what happened to me in my youth get in the way of my making a commitment to her. I became distant. I purposely pushed her further and further away. To the point where I destroyed our relationship."

"That's why you left the Center," Francy said. "I wondered. I couldn't believe you'd abandon John and Lucy."

"Yes, Francy, that's why I left. As I said, I was a coward."

"Why did you come back?" Sam asked.

"Because I thought Maddie was gone. I didn't know she'd been hired for John's job when I took the position of teen counselor or that she'd be my boss when I returned."

An uncomfortable silence now. That was new information to most of them.

"When I got back here, I managed to screw things up again with Maddie."

Utter silence in the room. Only the ringing of a phone down the hall and the sound of traffic outside the window could be heard.

"But yesterday taught me some things, as I imagine it did all of you." Now he spoke to her directly. "What I learned is that I want another chance. Maddie, I went to see my parents this morning."

At the other end of the table, she gasped and put a hand to her mouth.

"Now I know I'm the right man for you. Let me prove it. I want the whole shebang. Marriage, a kid or two. We're not too old yet…"

Uh-oh, she wasn't saying anything.

"I, um, figured if I confessed all, publicly, you'd be more likely to say yes."

Her eyes got bright with tears.

"You know how I hate this kind of thing." He shrugged boyishly. "Help me out here, love."

Her smile came then, big and beautiful. "I hate to resort to movie clichés, Nick, but you had me at hello."

It took him a minute to realize she was saying yes. "Well, I'll be damned."

He stood as she did. They met halfway around the table. Grabbing her to him, he kissed her hard, then leaned over and scooped her up in his arms. He headed for the door, with her face buried in his chest.

"Hey, where you going?" Beth asked.

"To finish groveling. Now that I know I don't have to do it in front of all of you."

They reached the door when Sam called out, "No fair. We should get to see the happily-ever-after."

Together, Nick and Maddie said, "You will!"

Nick kissed her head. "For the rest of our lives."

* * * * *

Mediterranean Nights

Join the guests and crew of Alexandra's Dream, *the newest luxury ship to set sail on the romantic Mediterranean, as they experience the glamorous world of cruising.*

A new Harlequin continuity series begins in June 2007 with
FROM RUSSIA, WITH LOVE
by Ingrid Weaver.

Marina Artamova books a cabin on the luxurious cruise ship Alexandra's Dream, *when she finds out that her orphaned nephew and his adoptive father are aboard. She's determined to be reunited with the boy…but the romantic ambience of the ship and her undeniable attraction to a man she considers her enemy are about to interfere with her quest!*

Turn the page for a sneak preview!

Piraeus, Greece

"THERE SHE IS, Stefan. *Alexandra's Dream.*" David Anderson squatted beside his new son and pointed at the dark blue hull that towered above the pier. The cruise ship was a majestic sight, twelve decks high and as long as a city block. A circle of silver and gold stars, the logo of the Liberty cruise line, gleamed from the swept-back smokestack. Like some legendary sea creature born for the water, the ship emanated power from every sleek curve—even at rest it held the promise of motion. "That's going to be our home for the next ten days."

The child beside him remained silent, his cheeks working in and out as he sucked furiously on his thumb. Hair so blond it appeared white ruffled against his forehead in the harbor breeze. The baby-sweet scent unique to the very young mingled with the tang of the sea.

"Ship," David said. "Uh, *parakhod.*"

From beneath his bangs, Stefan looked at the *Alexandra's Dream.* Although he didn't release his thumb, the corners of his mouth tightened with the beginning of a smile.

David grinned. That was Stefan's first smile this afternoon, one of only two since they had left the orphanage yesterday. It was probably because of the boat. According to the orphanage staff, the boy loved boats, which was the main reason David had decided to book this cruise. Then again, there was a strong possibility the smile could have been a reaction to David's attempt at pocket-dictionary Russian. Whatever the cause, it was a good start.

The liaison from the adoption agency had claimed that Stefan had been taught some English, but David had yet to see evidence of it. David continued to speak, positive his son would understand his tone even if he couldn't grasp the words. "This is her maiden voyage. Her first trip, just like this is our first trip, and that makes it special." He motioned toward the stage that had been set up on the pier beneath the ship's bow. "That's why everyone's celebrating."

The ship's official christening ceremony had been held the day before and had been a closed affair, with only the cruise-line executives and VIP guests invited, but the stage hadn't yet been disassembled. Banners bearing the blue and white of the Greek flag of the ship's owner, as well as the Liberty circle of stars logo, draped the edges of the platform. In the center, a group of musicians and a dance troupe dressed in traditional white folk costumes performed for the benefit of the *Alexan-*

dra's Dream's first passengers. Their audience was in a festive mood, snapping their fingers in time to the music while the dancers twirled and wove through their steps.

David bobbed his head to the rhythm of the mandolins. They were playing a folk tune that seemed vaguely familiar, possibly from a movie he'd seen. He hummed a few notes. "Catchy melody, isn't it?"

Stefan turned his gaze on David. His eyes were a striking shade of blue, as cool and pale as a winter horizon and far too solemn for a child not yet five. Still, the smile that hovered at the corners of his mouth persisted. He moved his head with the music, mirroring David's motion.

David gave a silent cheer at the interaction. Hopefully, this cruise would provide countless opportunities for more. "Hey, good for you," he said. "Do you like the music?"

The child's eyes sparked. He withdrew his thumb with a pop. *"Moozika!"*

"Music. Right!" David held out his hand. "Come on, let's go closer so we can watch the dancers."

Stefan grasped David's hand quickly, as if he feared it would be withdrawn. In an instant his budding smile was replaced by a look close to panic.

Did he remember the car accident that had killed his parents? It would be a mercy if he didn't. As far as David knew, Stefan had never spoken of it to anyone. Whatever he had seen had made him run so far from the crash that the police hadn't found him until the next day. The event had traumatized him to the extent that he hadn't uttered a word until his fifth week at the orphanage. Even now he seldom talked.

David sat back on his heels and brushed the hair from Stefan's forehead. That solemn, too-old gaze locked with his and, for an instant, David felt as if he looked back in time at an image of himself thirty years ago.

He didn't need to speak the same language to understand exactly how this boy felt. He knew what it meant to be alone and powerless among strangers, trying to be brave and tough but wishing with every fiber of his being for a place to belong, to be safe and, most of all, for someone to love him....

He knew in his heart he would be a good parent to Stefan. It was why he had never considered halting the adoption process after Ellie had left him. He hadn't balked when he'd learned of the recent claim by Stefan's spinster aunt, either; the absentee relative had shown up too late for her case to be considered. The adoption was meant to be. He and this child already shared a bond that went deeper than paperwork or legalities.

A seagull screeched overhead, making Stefan start and press closer to David.

"That's my boy," David murmured. He swallowed hard, struck by the simple truth of what he had just said.

That's my *boy.*

"I CAN'T BE PATIENT, RUDOLPH. I'm not going to stand by and watch my nephew get ripped from his country and his roots to live on the other side of the world."

Rudolph hissed out a slow breath. "Marina, I don't like the sound of that. What are you planning?"

"I'm going to talk some sense into this American kidnapper."

"No. Absolutely not. No offense, but diplomacy is not your strong suit."

"Diplomacy be damned. Their ship's due to sail at five o'clock."

"Then you wouldn't have an opportunity to speak with him even if his lawyer agreed to a meeting."

"I'll have ten days of opportunities, Rudolph, since I plan to be on board that ship."

* * * * *

*Follow Marina and David as they join forces
to uncover the reason behind little Stefan's unusual
silence and the secret behind the death
of his parents....*

*Look for FROM RUSSIA, WITH LOVE
by Ingrid Weaver
in stores June 2007.*

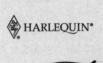

Silhouette®
ROMANTIC
SUSPENSE

**Sparked *by* Danger,
Fueled *by* Passion.**

*This month and every month look for
four new heart-racing romances
set against a backdrop of suspense!*

Available in June 2007

Shelter from the Storm
by RaeAnne Thayne

A Little Bit Guilty
(Midnight Secrets miniseries)
by Jenna Mills

Mob Mistress
by Sheri WhiteFeather

A Serial Affair
by Natalie Dunbar

Available wherever you buy books!

Visit Silhouette Books at www.eHarlequin.com SRS0507

REQUEST YOUR FREE BOOKS!
2 FREE NOVELS PLUS 2 FREE GIFTS!

HARLEQUIN®

Super Romance®

Exciting, emotional, unexpected!

YES! Please send me 2 FREE Harlequin Superromance® novels and my 2 FREE gifts. After receiving them, if I don't wish to receive any more books, I can return the shipping statement marked "cancel." If I don't cancel, I will receive 6 brand-new novels every month and be billed just $4.69 per book in the U.S., or $5.24 per book in Canada, plus 25¢ shipping and handling per book and applicable taxes, if any*. That's a savings of close to 15% off the cover price! I understand that accepting the 2 free books and gifts places me under no obligation to buy anything. I can always return a shipment and cancel at any time. Even if I never buy another book from Harlequin, the two free books and gifts are mine to keep forever.

135 HDN EEX7   336 HDN EEYK

Name	(PLEASE PRINT)	

Address		Apt.

City	State/Prov.	Zip/Postal Code

Signature (if under 18, a parent or guardian must sign)

Mail to the Harlequin Reader Service®:
IN U.S.A.: P.O. Box 1867, Buffalo, NY 14240-1867
IN CANADA: P.O. Box 609, Fort Erie, Ontario L2A 5X3

Not valid to current Harlequin Superromance subscribers.

Want to try two free books from another line?
Call 1-800-873-8635 or visit www.morefreebooks.com.

* Terms and prices subject to change without notice. NY residents add applicable sales tax. Canadian residents will be charged applicable provincial taxes and GST. This offer is limited to one order per household. All orders subject to approval. Credit or debit balances in a customer's account(s) may be offset by any other outstanding balance owed by or to the customer. Please allow 4 to 6 weeks for delivery.

Your Privacy: Harlequin is committed to protecting your privacy. Our Privacy Policy is available online at www.eHarlequin.com or upon request from the Reader Service. From time to time we make our lists of customers available to reputable firms who may have a product or service of interest to you. If you would prefer we not share your name and address, please check here. ☐

HSR0

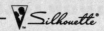

SPECIAL EDITION™

COMING IN JUNE

HER LAST FIRST DATE

by *USA TODAY* bestsellling author

SUSAN MALLERY

After one too many bad dates, Crissy Phillips
finally swore off men. Recently widowed,
pediatrician Josh Daniels can't risk losing his
heart. With an intense attraction pulling them
together, will their fear keep them apart?
Or will one wild night change everything…?

**Sometimes the unexpected
is the best news of all….**

HARLEQUIN

Super Romance®

COMING NEXT MONTH

#1422 COULDA BEEN A COWBOY • Brenda Novak
A Dundee, Idaho story

Tyson Garnier is a stranger to Dundee—and to his own infant son. The baby was
neglected by his mother, so Tyson paid her off to get full custody. Now he needs a
temporary nanny, and Dakota Brown is perfect. She's completely unlike the kind of
women Tyson usually attracts. She's poor, a little plain, a hard worker. Who would've
guessed he'd find himself falling for someone like *that*?

#1423 BLAME IT ON THE DOG • Amy Frazier
Singles...with Kids

An out-of-control mutt. A preteen son. Dog trainer Jack Quinn. These are the males i
Selena Milano's life. The first two she loves. The third? Who knows? But he sure do
make things interesting.

#1424 HIS PERFECT WOMAN • Kay Stockham

Dr. Bryan Booker is the perfect man. Ask almost every woman in town—including
some of the married ones. Even Melissa York is hard-pressed to deny Bryan's charm
Not that she can afford to be interested...since he's already said the only way she can
work for him is if they keep everything professional. But is he going to remember th

#1425 DAD FOR LIFE • Helen Brenna
A Little Secret

Lucas Rydall is looking for redemption. His search leads him to his ex-wife,
Sydney Mitchell—and the son he didn't know he had. But his discovery puts them
all in danger. To save his family, Lucas must put aside his fears and become the man
his family needs.

#1426 MR. IRRESISTIBLE • Karina Bliss

Entrepreneur Jordan King is handsome and charismatic, and he's used to getting any
woman he wants. Until journalist Kate Brogan catches his eye—and refuses to give
to her obvious feelings for him. Because the way she sees it, he's just like her father
a no-good philanderer at the mercy of his passions. So all Jordan has to do is convin
her he's utterly irresistible.

#1427 WANTED MAN • Ellen K. Hartman

Nathan has a secret. One he has to hide—which means leaving his old life behind an
not telling a soul who he really is. But how can a man with any honor even think ab
getting involved with a woman as wonderful as Rhian MacGregor?

HSRCNM0507